Darkening Danger

Sammy Sutton

Enjoy the experience!

Sammy Sutton

DEDICATION

This story is for those who spend their professional lives exploring the
unknown...

Special Thanks to Kathy Feigel & Ethan Feigel for their contributions.

iv

ALSO BY SAMMY SUTTON

King Solomon's Journey

Hidden Mountain

Reliquary of Dimensions

Upcoming Concealed

Disclaimer

Darkening Danger *is a work of fiction. All events are products of the author's imagination. Any similarities to real people or situations are purely coincidental.*

Chapter 1

Miami, Florida

Michael Levine

The void of darkness is surrounding me. My naked skin beaded with moisture chills to the bone. The perfect darkness elicits no sound except my own heartbeat and heavy breathing, no smells, and except for the company of my own fear, I am alone. From the darkness comes a light that separates and splits into innumerable floating squares. I am watching as they begin to move and oscillate around me, faster and faster... Reaching out to catch one, my hand is passing through its center, and I see each transparent slip of light is actually a formula or equation. All of the answers sought by scientists and mathematicians are within my reach, but I can't grasp one of them! What does this mean and why is it so damn familiar?

So many numbers are passing by I can't focus on one group. Out of the oblivion comes a backdrop to the equation, photographic flashes of famine and devastation have me struggling not to close my eyes. The gray and white images of the sunken eyed people are frightening. Compounding my fears are the visions of the gruesome dry deserted terrain scattered with animal skeletons. Out of a squint, I look to see post-apocalyptic images...oh God, is it the past or the future? I can't be sure. It reminds me of photos shot by Rothstein or Lange of the economic disaster during WWII and the famous western droughts. Somehow a part of me knows this is the foreboding future mankind will face in the wake of the sun's hiatus.

Sickened, giving into the pain, I double over and recognize the familiar darkened surroundings of my bedroom in Miami. I stumble in an awkward race to open the blackout drapes covering the French doors, and in a state of madness, I pull them back and breathe a sigh of relief at the sight of the fiery ball rising above the blue waters of the Atlantic Ocean. I swing open the doors, walk out onto the veranda, and soak in the heat of the rays.

Quickly, I decide to shower and return to The National Oceanic and Atmospheric Association (NOAA). I just left there a few hours ago, but the circumstances demands I return before my flight back to my more permanent residence in Corpus Christi. My family lives there, and I am anxious to enjoy Thanksgiving with my relatives.

Waiting for the shower to warm, I think back to my days at MIT as a young student hungry for answers to questions. Today, as if the dream were a portent, my wish is for an unintelligent normalcy.

In record time, I'm showered, dressed, a short drive later and I wave at the security guard as I pass through the gate. I swiftly maneuver my car into my marked spot and make my way into the building to my office. Considered a senior member of the team, I am actually a contracted consultant. Having made the point, recently NOAA and the issues at hand have demanded far more of my attention than usual.

Inside my office I buzz for Clyde, one of three intern assistants assigned by NOAA. I need coffee and the latest data sets. I pull the most recent research from the shelves and turn back to my desk to find myself face to face with none other than the current bane of my professional life, Dr. Larson Taylor.

"Ever hear of knocking Larson?"

Why knock, the door was open." The muted tones of an expensive suit go well with the distinguished appearance of the man who just barged into my office. Yet, the Wall Street Banker appearance of Larson doesn't fool me one bit.

"What do you want?" I ask resignedly.

"Just to let you know that young geologist…what's his name Raymond?"

"Ryan, his name as you very well know is, Ryan."

"Yes, well whatever. He totally screwed the pooch in Washington yesterday. Those people will never listen to us again!"

"What are you talking about?"

"I thought you knew. I took young Ryan with me to address

the Hill, yesterday. I did my best Michael, but they refused to listen to me. Especially after young Ryan gave them the horror story version of what to expect in the near future. Of course, with no scientific proof to back up his claims, they refused to hear me out."

His words have me clinching my teeth and my fist.

"That meeting was scheduled for Monday, why did you go yesterday, with Ryan and without me?" I ask the smirking man now lounging across from me.

"I received a personal invitation from the Chairman, and of course I couldn't say no. Besides, what could you tell them that I could not?"

"A great deal and you know it, Larson! This project has been under my supervision since NOAA decided to use my equipment to track these atmospheric changes!"

With a wave of his finely manicured hand, Larson dismisses my answer. He stands, straightens his cuffs, and makes his way to the door. His parting shot has me wishing I was a less civilized man;

"My point in coming here this morning was to tell you that your protégé ruined it for us. I expect you to take care of this issue, immediately."

Clyde passes him on the way in with my coffee, and I order him to find Ryan and send him to me, now.

So much rested on that meeting on the Hill, and now the opportunity was lost. I drop into my chair and just sit there, staring at the stack of now useless data that I intended to present to those who could have made a difference in Washington.

A soft knock announces the arrival of Ryan, and not surprisingly Mary is with him. She is Ryan's opposite in almost every way, yet lately she seems to always be close at hand when Ryan is around.

They both stand just inside the door, like wary children called to the principal's office; their brilliant minds overshadowed by their social ineptness. Mary dresses down the natural beauty of her image and seems determined to appear as unassuming as possible, while Ryan could care less about his appearance or anyone else's opinion, except when his reputation or qualifications are in question. Ryan's brusque manner and tendency to answer others questions in a 'how dumb can you be' tone often leave him standing outside of the cliques that tend to form within think tanks like NOAA. He can't seem to recognize that others aren't capable of grasping new ideas and data as fast as he can.

Where Mary's shyness often prevents her from gaining the recognition she deserves, Ryan's seemingly defiant attitude keeps him out of the running for higher placement.

"Ryan, would you care to explain why you accompanied Larson to Washington days earlier than planned and without telling me?" I demand.

"He lied to me, Michael. He said you were meeting us there and bringing the data. Once we arrived, he took my cell phone, my laptop and refused to allow me to speak to anyone…said it was a directive from the Chairman for security purposes."

"Why does that not surprise me in the least?" An ugly laugh escapes me as I stare at the earnest face of one of the most brilliant young men, I have ever met. He began to pace in front of my desk, words spewing out in staccato burst.

"Slow down Ryan, and tell me what happened."

I watch as Ryan stopped, took deep breaths and composed himself.

"When we were before the committee, he introduced me and threw me under the bus. With no hard data, I had no way to explain or back-up what we have discovered. They laughed at me Michael. They said I should be in Hollywood, writing for science-fiction movies!"

"What did Larson do?"

"He told them that yes, there were some atmospheric changes and that there could be sun-spots, slight changes in the tides, and perhaps a few earlier hours each day of deepening twilight, as well as a brilliant meteor shower and that we would let them know in a few months if we discovered any other developments. He apologized to them for my ineptitude and said he had been told I was the best you had to offer."

Boiling mad, does not even come close to describing the level of anger building inside me. I slam back in my chair, rise and storm out the door, and down the hall to Larson's office. His secretary stops me from storming into his office.

"Dr. Levine he's not there! He left right after he came back from your office, he told me to cancel his meetings until after Thanksgiving. I'm sorry sir, but he's already left the building."

"Do you know where he's gone?"

"I made arrangements early this morning for him to return to Washington…with a return flight Monday evening. That's all I know sir."

"Alright Jenny, if he contacts you let him know, I will be waiting to see him when he returns."

My smile must be ugly, poor Jenny is clutching her blouse front as she stammers a soft, yes sir.

Walking slowly back down the hall, my thoughts return to my dream. If the equations were correct, this disaster with Larson could force an outcome far worse than I imagined yesterday.

A shy voice is calling my name. Looking up, I see Mary waiting for me.

"Dr. Levine, sorry to bother you, but can I show you something?"

"Is it important Mary?"

"I believe so sir."

"Then do not apologize, just show me."

"If you will come to the lab, I have additional information I haven't shared with anyone else."

This is Mary's way of saying she has left Larson out of the loop, again. Technically she works for him, not me, but since my arrival she has come to me more and more. At first I had been afraid she was infatuated with me...then a blow to my ego when I discovered, she simply thought I was the smarter man with fewer personal agendas.

Eight months earlier, Ryan had come to me after one of my new programs had detected an explosion in space. A rogue Centaur asteroid had collided with the Jovian asteroid cloud near Jupiter, and the collision had been enormous. Since over the last few decades our views of the Jovian asteroid clouds was limited to the northern skies at certain times of the year, this collision at the right time had generated enormous excitement.

Over the last few months, we had watched as the debris cloud made up of harder materials from the asteroids had coalesced, thanks to gravitational tugs into a moving disk, it had now formed into a large gaseous cloud that was picking up all debris in its path.

Once we enter Mary's lab, she shoos out the other techies and closes the door. From a locked drawer, she draws forth a disc and inserts it into the three-dimensional viewing table.

I watch as the program correlates data and formulates a tracking model of the suns movements over the next thirty days.

"I cannot guarantee the exact time sir…but sometime in the next week or so we are looking at the extreme possibility that the debris cloud, or as Ryan calls it the 'Levine Wave', that we have been observing will not pass Earth safely, but will most likely pass between the Earth and moon. The models are forecasting extreme atmospheric changes that could last anywhere from 72-80 hours. I can't be any clearer on the time as of yet, but Sir, this will not remain a secret; astronomers around the world will see it and word will spread. How are we supposed to warn the public, and if we do, what do we tell them?"

Mary's concern is real and her confusion understandable. Releasing this information in the wrong way will create public panic. Damn Larson for blowing what might have been our only real chance to stop the hysteria from happening.

The information we collected tells us that this cloud is heading towards Earth's atmosphere and will cause a massive meteor shower, some of the larger debris could impact land masses and sea areas, and will knock out satellites around the globe. I cringe at the thought of the future once acid rain washes the Earth for days, along with a few billion tons of rock debris and gaseous cloud elements; this coupled with no communication, lasting darkness, and an inability to cope without their normal daily routines will impact people drastically. The cloud of falling meteoroids, debris, and rock will block out quality light for days, all while intermittent alarming fireworks explode in the skies overhead.

"Since we made this discovery Mary, you have been on top of it. Do your best now to try and discover a closer time-frame to predict the arrival of the cloud, if we can't avoid it, we can do our best to prepare as many as possible for it."

"After what happened in Washington sir, will they listen now?"

"Probably not, but I still have a few friends I can call in for help if we have time. Make a copy of what we have so far, including this new material and get it over to Gary Timmons at NASA. I will call him later and find out if they have anything to share."

"Yes sir."

"Do you have family Mary?"

"A sister out in Des Moines, that's all."

"Call her Mary, tell her what we know."

"I will tonight. If it's all the same to you sir...I have no plans for the Holidays and will stay here working."

"I hate to see you do that Mary, but I have to go...I have quite a few businesses to prepare and relatives to get moving on preparation as well."

"Umm, Ryan volunteered for duty this week so he will be here also. Between us, we can gather twice the information!"

"Alright then, call me and let me know any new developments. Call maintenance Mary and have them change the locks on these doors, not that I mistrust anyone in particular...but better safe than sorry when you're holding explosive materials."

Mary nods and I watch her head for the phone. Leaving her office, I seek out Ryan to no avail. He has gone deeper into the labyrinth of NOAA and will only surface when he is sure it is safe to do so. I shrug, out of time; I gather my things and head for the airport.

Stuck in a traffic jam, it seems everyone is rushing to Miami International Airport. With no movement on the interstate, I relax into the car's seat. A prism of light from the sun bounces off the car in front of me, and a name comes to mind, Brandon Lewis, a former Texas A&M graduate student. Brandon never officially received his PhD, at least in person. Instead, the department awarded it in his honor to his grieving mother. Word has it, his use of hallucinogens resulted in an accidental suicide. His work was either brilliant or crazy, when I read it the first time the latter came to mind, recent events have me thinking otherwise. Making a mental note, I decide after the Thanksgiving weekend, I will retrieve a copy from the repository in Corpus Christi.

Inside the airport lounge, I ask for a double shot of bourbon with a Heineken back. Thoughts of my personal aloneness intertwine with the catastrophe now hanging over the Earth. Long ago, I prepared myself and my relatives for just such an event. Everything is in place except the companion...sure there's James, but there hasn't truly been a woman since Sabine.

My current sometime relationship with Kim, the high-strung and pretentious real estate broker, is embarrassing at best. The last time we were together, I wasn't sure if I could make it through dinner. In fact, I feigned a call in the middle of the entrée and excused myself to tend to urgent business. Kim doesn't understand what I do and appears bored with even casual conversation about my profession. At this moment, I miss Sabine more than ever. She was a budding archeologist in those days, and despite all that was wrong in our relationship, she understood me as a scientist. I slam down the last of the Heineken and contemplate another, when halted by the call to board, I abandon my thoughts.

Chapter 2

Corpus Christi, Texas

Johanna Mueller

Moving forward, my footsteps echo hollowly on the marble floor, the sound is as hollow as my emotions have become. That is except for fear, fear is now my constant companion; and yes, approaching the counter in this repository is scaring the hell out of me. The idea of having to appear carefree and jovial even for a few moments has me frightened to my very core. Despite actually being here for more than a month, this is my first excursion alone in this city.

The older stereotypical librarian is far from a frightening specter, yet my breath catches in my throat as she asks what she can do for me. For a moment, I freeze before mustering a grin and handing her a piece of paper with the titles of the two dissertations; my need for the information those dissertations may contain has forced me into a situation I dread.

My request for copies is barely audible, and her large grin catches me off guard. Returning the smile feels forced and fake, yet I must play the game. She turns around to face the computer monitor situated opposite of the large mahogany counter.

My eyes shift to the stunning tall man leaning against the

circular counter. His dark hair graying ever so slightly at the temples gives him a distinguished appearance. He nods at me with a warm smile that nearly knocks the breath right out me. Hollowed out yes; dead from the neck down, no! I've been away from life entirely too long. Whoa!

Not wanting to draw attention, my nod in return is shallow and brief, quickly turning my gaze back to face the librarian. After a few seconds, the pleasant woman turns towards me.

"What is your name dear?"

I nearly panic; my name? Oh damn, I hesitate. She's staring at me.

"Jill Maddux." Another forced smile and my face feels as if it will crack with the effort.

Feeling stupid, I catch another glimpse at the man standing a couple of feet away from me. He seems amused by something, and it might very well be me. I'm making a spectacle of myself. I am not a teenager skipping school, and this nervousness must come across as ridiculous.

The woman twirls around and looks at me from across the counter. "I'm so sorry Ms. Maddux; I can't locate you in the computer. Communication with the main campus today is sporadic at best. I will need your faculty or student identification card."

16

Damnation; red tape and rules everywhere! With a stronger more assured voice, I respond. "I'm sorry, I thought I could simply pay for copies, I didn't realize there would be a need to be affiliated with the University, please forgive my ignorance."

The librarian smiles, and says honestly; "It's okay dear, if it were my choice I would be more than happy to give you the copies." This time my polite grin is not forced. "I understand, but can you help me with some directions?"

"Sure, I'm more than happy to help."

In a forced lighthearted voice, I ask. "A coffee shop, you know the kind that conjures up those really frothy, chocolaty coffee drinks." Nothing deceptive here, deprived long enough, I am craving a rich coffee beverage.

She giggles and directs me to the campus Starbucks. My exit is not as smooth as I had wished, my turn is jerky and my feet are clumsy! To think these same feet once graced the smooth floors of Miss Anna's Dance Studio! Where has all the grace gone?

My eyes catch one more look at the man staring and clearly laughing at my inability to not only know my own name, but an inability to walk like an adult as well. Barely able to control my urge to stick out my tongue, I give him a haughty look and walk as quickly as possible to the exit.

Michael Levine

As I watch the strange woman rush out the door I shake my head, her demeanor has certainly peaked my interest. Suspecting she needs the dissertations for a good reason, I turn and with a smile address Laverne.

"Laverne, print the copies the peculiar Ms. Maddux wants, and put it under my name."

She smiles back at me. "Of course, Dr. Levine, I will be happy to oblige. Is there anything else I can copy for you?"

I smile; "No thank you, I will return later, I think I need to move fast to catch up at the coffee house with the elusive Ms. Maddux." I give an imaginary twist to an imaginary moustache, and tip an imaginary hat and Laverne giggles, hands me the copies and I thank her.

James would be so proud of me! I hadn't made the older woman nervous nor think me to be rude. Rolling my eyes at my thoughts and my behavior, I take giant strides in the direction of the Starbucks while scanning the dissertations. Why in the hell would the woman be interested in such a detailed scientific report about magnetic dip?

I give an evil chuckle as I peer through the glass and spot the shoulder length dark hair belonging to Jill Maddux. The woman now seated at a table, is pulling a notepad from her attaché.

Approaching from behind, I inquire softly. "Jill Maddux." The woman doesn't flinch. She is writing something on her notepad. Moving around to the side of the table I repeat her name. "Ms. Maddux." Again, she doesn't acknowledge me. What is she, deaf? Moving closer, I raise my voice slightly. "Jill Maddux."

She jumps visibly before her head pops up with a bewildered look in her eyes. Holding my position, I hold out the folder; "Ms. Maddux, I secured the dissertation copies you wanted under my name."

The woman is frozen. Her wide eyed look is almost frantic. I watch as her gorgeous eyes dance around the nearly deserted coffee shop. "Thank you sir, but I couldn't accept such a gesture."

Why the hell not? My charity should have earned me at least the opportunity to enjoy a cup of coffee with the woman, but now the thought seems unrealistic. The woman is clearly uncomfortable and it doesn't seem to necessarily be from my presence.

"Ms. Maddux, I assure you I am safe and mean you no harm."

"Said Ted Bundy; over and over again to young women for years."

"Ms. Maddux, you can rest assured, I am no serial killer!" My affronted outburst elicits another quick glance around the room

19

from her.

"Mister, quit saying my name."

What in the hell? Taking a chance, I boldly take a seat in the empty chair at the table with her. Keeping my voice at a hushed and unthreatening level, I introduce myself. "My name is Michael Levine...Dr. Michael Levine. You seem to be afraid of something, can I help you?"

She snaps out her words. "I don't need a doctor."

"Don't worry, I'm not a medical doctor; I am a geophysicist."

She stares at me with a glimmer of interest. "Really?"

A young male barista interrupts the moment, and sets the giant coffee drink in front of Jill.

"Sir, what can I get started for you?"

Making eye contact with Jill, I decide, I am staying. She will have to create a scene to get me to move, now; "Just plain coffee."

"You should try one of the blends; the flavors are bold and impertinent." Jill suggests.

"Just like me, huh?"

Her blush is my reward as I call her out on her remarks.

She glances out the window, and I turn my head to see what has caught her attention. A young boy is walking past with a hand holding tight to the string of a balloon. It's a beautiful clear day outside, yet in an instant the indoor lights flicker, suddenly the outdoors darkens ever so slightly, and everyone pauses. My muscles tighten in anticipation, another warning has come. Within seconds, things lighten back up, and the people seem to shrug and go back to their business.

Turning back to Jill I see her eyes searching the horizon for storm clouds; not gonna find them. Her momentary distraction allows me to take a closer look without appearing to be the pervert she hinted I am.

Smartly dressed, her black pants lay smooth against her thin yet, curvy figure. The snug, white button-up blouse is a quality design that doesn't attempt to hide her ample breasts. She has soft, supple skin, but I would guess that is due more too careful care rather than a true indicator of a younger age.

When the barista places my coffee on the table, she jerks and looks back at me. For a moment she forgot I was here! Her eyes once more hold that lost look and her stiff posture speaks of fear, ready to take flight.

Stirring my coffee, allows me to speak without looking up at her. "The papers are for you, and it is no problem. No strings attached." Hesitating, approaching the subject softly and slowly, I make my observations as least threatening as possible.

"I feel that you believe you are in danger. I would like to help."

"Thank you, but I am fine. You see I have only recently moved

21

here and I am a bit disoriented." She gives me a forced smile that is not very convincing.

Making eye contact for a brief moment, I am convinced the woman sitting before me does not fit her paranoid behavior; let's try a new approach. As she takes a sip from her cup, I clear my throat, and try for a more casual conversation.

"So what brings you to Corpus Christi?"
Again her eyes widen, but her body language relaxes with the less personal question. "The water, I am very fond of the beach."

It feels like progress. "I assume where you are from there are no beaches, where might that be?"

Jill shifts her weight and seems to wiggle ever so slightly. "I'm from Chicago."

Well that tells me one thing, she can't lie convincingly. I know full well this woman is not, at least originally from Chicago. Although not pronounced, I can detect a slight eastern accent. "I take it Lake Michigan is not your idea of an acceptable body of water?"

Apparently, she finds this observation genuinely funny and forgets her plight. A refreshing giggle escapes her. "No, I'm afraid for a beach lover the Gulf is a much kinder body of water."

"Well, I suppose I can't argue with you over that point; unless of course it's hurricane season."

She relaxes her tense shoulders ever so slightly and takes a couple more sips of her elaborate coffee beverage. Catching her gaze, I smile warmly, which sends her in a rush to check her cell phone. She begins stuffing her notebook back into the attaché. "I really must go, Dr. Levine." She removes a wallet from her purse.

Wanting only to stay her hand at the fumble for money for the check, I reach out and my slight touch sends her into a tailspin and she jumps as if touched by a live wire. Continuing, pretending not to notice the over-reaction, I offer; "Please, call me Michael and I will pay for our coffee. I insist."

With her wallet lying open, it's easy for me to glance down at her driver's license. She's already secured a Texas license. In a flash, she swipes up the wallet and Jill Maddux is racing out the door. After hastily throwing down enough to cover the bill, I rush out to try and catch up with the ditzy woman!

Careful not to say her name, I call after her. "Please, take the dissertations." She seems to not hear or ignores my pleas. Defeated, for the moment, all I can do is shake my head, and return to the repository to retrieve the information I came for in the first place.

Chapter 3

I lean back in my chair staring at the papers on my desk intended for Jill Maddux. A few days ago, after memorizing the address on her driver's license, I felt confident I would be able to secure a phone number for the damn crazy woman, but instead, every trick I employed met with a dead end. Baffled by defeat, in one quick move, I snatch the papers off my desk, stand and stomp out of my office.

My longtime assistant Diana is calling after me. "Dr. Levine will you be returning?"

I bark back at her. "With any luck... no."

Inside the private parking garage James, my driver and personal all around man, spots me and is moving quickly towards the black SUV. I dismiss him with a wave. "I'll drive myself."

I slide into the black ML-63, tear out of the garage, and begin reprimanding my behavior. "What kind of a dumb son of a bitch am I? She's a paranoid nut. If she really wanted the papers she would have taken them when I offered."

"Not like I have nothing else planned today!" I say sarcastically to my image in the rearview mirror.

With a swift look at the dash, I see it's almost 4:00 pm. So much for my carefully laid plans, I think about; an evening commitment at the club, with a date; Kim, and I am racing to check on a woman whose behavior, interests, and overall demeanor defies all logic.

Conveniently, not far from MLE, 'Michael Levine Enterprises', I locate a meticulous two story adobe with an abundance of colorful landscaping. Not a design I would expect belonged to a clinically delusional woman. I grumble under my breath, the mysterious woman has already taken entirely too much energy. Exiting the SUV, I walk up the patterned red brick path leading to the entryway, and ring the doorbell. The sound coming from inside assures someone, hopefully Jill, is looking to see who's at the door.

Finally, the door opens. I catch myself staring at the stunning woman standing in the doorway. Her beautiful red polished toes and shapely bare legs are completely visible below the equally impressive short sundress. The sight of her naked arms has me taking a deep breath.

"Dr. Levine?"

I regain my composure, and refuse to appear affected. "I want you to have these papers." I murmur in an authoritative tone. Jill stares at me. Not exactly relaxed, even so, she is much more at ease than the first time we met. Her smile lights up her face. "You should not have gone to all this trouble."

Knowing she has a point, in a tone more sarcastic than I intend, I reply. "Well I did, and in return I would appreciate it if you would take the copies and invite me inside for a drink."

Despite my harshness, she seems to be contemplating my suggestion, but then hesitates. I react quickly before she has a chance to refuse. "If that idea would upset your husband then let me take you to a public place for a drink or coffee."

Her hand moves to her mouth as if to hide her grin. "Of course, please come inside." I follow her across the threshold and into the stone floored foyer.

She turns to me, her flushed face assures, she is embarrassed. Her voice is soft and sweet. "Dr. Levine…Michael, I'm afraid I have yet to purchase many furnishings and household items. In fact, the best I can offer is some cranberry juice in a coffee mug."

I smirk. "Fine then, I choose cranberry juice."

She turns leading me into an impressive kitchen with only a coffee pot and a couple barstools as proof someone is making use of the space. The arrangement supports the idea, something very peculiar is going on with this woman. She isn't a college student, where in the hell is her stuff?

"Ms. Maddux, how long have you been in Corpus?" My curiosity is untamable.

She doesn't turn to face me as she answers; instead she busies

26

herself pouring cranberry juice into a couple of coffee mugs. "Please call me Jill. I arrived here about a month ago."

I continue to pry. "What do you do, Jill?"

She sets the juice down, and pauses before answering my question. "I paint, I'm afraid I'm not Rembrandt, but I do enjoy it."

The woman couldn't tell the truth if she had to, so why am I not leaving? Annoyed with my intense curiosity, I decide to try to initiate some idle conversation. Maybe, I can gain her trust. "Well, I assume you have spent a great deal of your time at the beach since your arrival." She sure hasn't used her time shopping.

Her expression suddenly grows sad. "No, I am afraid I have not yet visited the beach." Her voice is soft.

Her reaction sends a pang in my stomach and an idea out of my damn mouth. "You know it is almost dinner time, and I'm guessing you have nothing in that refrigerator to eat. There is a great little place on the beach that serves the best fish tacos and margaritas in the United States. Let me take you there." I am shocked by my invitation.

I watch her eyes as they widen in response to my suggestion. "Jill, I'm not a threat."

She nods as if she knows this to be true, and then in a whisper she replies. "Okay."

27

Surprised, I rush to speak before she changes her mind. "Go get some shoes, and I will make a phone call, then we'll leave."

In slow motion, Jill exits the kitchen. I quickly dial Diana, she answers on the first ring. I tell her to call and cancel my evening commitments. Diana's voice is vibrating skepticism through my cell phone. My eyes roll. I must be mad. No it isn't Kim, certainly no love lost in that relationship. Kim, a convenience, I can live without. The question is; why does this woman and her odd situation, captivate me? Is it her or the information she sought at the repository? Maybe, it is the possibility that she is alone and in danger. I rub my hand across my forehead. Without delay, Jill re-enters the kitchen wearing sandals and thankfully she has not changed her dress. At least for now, I am sure my decision is the right one.

Engulfed in a sort of uncomfortable silence, we endure the short drive to the beach. At a loss for words, I am consciously aware of her discomfort and do not wish to exacerbate the problem.

Safely parked at Julio's On the Beach, I glance over at Jill. Already, she is staring out at the vast waters, obviously mesmerized by what she sees. I give her a moment before asking, "Jill, would you like to take a stroll along the beach before we eat?"

Like a much younger woman, in a higher pitch, she responds

with an undertone of excitement. "I would be most pleased to be allowed."

My forehead wrinkles. Allowed, what the hell is behind such an idea? But before I can say another word Jill rushes out of the vehicle leaving her purse and cell phone behind. I watch, at the edge of the sand, she halts to slip off her sandals. Amused, I mimic, and follow her to the ocean's edge.

Time passes, and I continue to watch the woman walk around the beach, periodically allowing the shimmering waves to bury her feet. The breeze is flowing through her soft hair, and every now and then, it catches her dress causing her to react quickly and grasp the sides tightly in her fists. She turns and I quickly snap a couple of pictures with my phone's camera. She doesn't appear to notice.

After a while, her eyes glowing, she stops to smile at me. "Thank you." Speechless, I nod, but move closer to join her near the water. As if she is returning to reality she speaks to me from an apologetic tone. "Michael you must be hungry; I'm sorry for the delay. The beauty is fascinating me. Julio's looks wonderful. Did I mention I love fish tacos?" She reaches out for my hand and leads me to the restaurant. I squint at her and accept.

We stop on the plank outside Julio's to dust the sand off our feet and put our shoes back on. Bemused, I open the door for her and we enter the casual Oceanside eatery.

"Hey, Dr. Levine, good to see you," Julio shouts from behind the bar.

I am smiling and waving. "Julio, I've brought my friend here for some of your famous fish tacos, and of course, margaritas."

"Good, Good, I'll get you fixed up, sit anywhere you like."

I nod, and lead Jill to a table overlooking the Gulf. Our eyes meet as I pull out the chair for her to sit. The sparkle in her eyes has me questioning how this could be the same woman that was so frightened a few days ago. Granted, she still isn't sharing any information about herself, but she's friendly and alive, and definitely seems to enjoy being here with me. I can't imagine what is so different, now.

Interrupting my private personal conversation, she asks. "Michael, are you teaching a lot of classes this semester?"

I laugh a bit. "I haven't taught since graduate school."

She looks confused, and I conclude her confusion must have something to do with the events at the repository. "I serve on a board at the university's main campus in Bryan Station that is why I have an identification that allows me to use the facilities. Actually, I'm a businessman, and from time to time I do some field work, if it interests me."

Her frown catches me off-guard. Her next words are perplexing. "I'm glad to know you do some hands-on work.

30

People know you around here?"

I smirk, and wonder why she cares about my work in the field, but for now, I am enjoying the fact that she isn't aware of whom I am or what I do. "I suppose they do. Jill, do you have friends or family here?"

She looks down. "No, except for one...I guess you could call him a friend."

Julio approaches our table with chips, salsa and a couple of magnificent margaritas. Not actually a drink I normally order, but they pair nicely with the fish tacos Julio prepares. The size of the margaritas gets a dramatic reaction from my companion.

"Oh my, you didn't tell me the margaritas were served out of a fish bowl. I don't often drink, this could be lethal."

I chuckle. "You're fine, drink as much as you like. I won't let anything happen to you." Inside, I'm reeling from the revelation; maybe she'll get drunk and start talking. She appears to genuinely appreciate my assurance as she smiles, places the straw between her luscious lips, and takes a big drink.

"Your friend..." She cuts off my words as if she is anticipating I might ask something she doesn't want to answer. "He said, he knew of you and believed you to be trustworthy, but added a strange disclosure. He said I would need to find out the rest on my own."

Semi-accolades from a stranger, but the revelation explains her change in demeanor. "What is your friend's name, perhaps I know him? What does he do?"

She blurts out as if prepared for the question. "Jack Jenkins, he is sort of a relocation specialist."

Hmm, the name seems vaguely familiar to me. No time to dwell though, she's talking, and drinking the margarita fairly quickly. A little too soon, Julio arrives with our fish tacos. They smell delicious and with the first bite Jill is enjoying the unique mixture of grilled fish, vegetables, and cilantro.

Nearly dark now, the crowd fills the moderate space. The patrons are drinking, eating, and dancing to a small ensemble playing a mixture of classic rock and country music. She is singing and swaying to the music from her seat, and oddly enough I feel content just watching her.

After several songs, and half of a second margarita she looks over at me. I hesitate, not in the habit of giving into this type of female whim; I stare at her, and decide to ask her the one question, I know she wants to hear me ask.

"Jill, do you want to dance with me?"

Her face lights up. "Yes." The word is coming out through a gasp.

Standing, I reach out to her. Jill's coy eyes move as if she is inspecting me for the first time. She accepts my hand. I look down at the woman as we wait for the next song. It begins, and I freeze, of course, '*At This Moment*' a song made famous by Billy Vera another lifetime ago, now only serving as a rude reminder of Sabine. I inhale, deep.

Trying to recover in the crowded dance area, I take Jill into my arms and move to the slow soft tune. She smells and feels like an angel swaying with me to the beat of the music, so reminiscent. At the end of the song, I pull back. I am shaking my head as I lead her back to the table. Jill's eyes widen in my direction. She whispers. "I'm sorry."

Oh God, what in the hell am I doing? I want her trust, but I'm falling for the nutty woman. Damn, I just wanted to know she was safe and give her the copies of the dissertations she needed. Now, I'm thinking of things, and she's insulted. I decide to try and explain, or at least provide an explanation she might understand. "Jill, I'm sorry, it's me. I'm not much of a dancer."

She smiles, but I see it does not meet her eyes. I try to placate. "How about another walk on the beach, I'm much better at that." She nods.

I settle our tab, and we saunter out onto the outside plank where again we remove our shoes. Cautiously, I take Jill's hand and we quietly enjoy the breeze, the lapping of the waves and the whispering sprays of the ocean.

Soon, she is shivering in the cool breeze. Placing my arm around her I pull her next to me. "I'm sorry Jill, it is November, and I should have told you to grab a jacket. It gets very chilly at night this close to the water."

"It's okay," she tries to assure.

"No, you're freezing, we need to go, understand I will bring you back whenever you want." My promise surprises both of us as we begin walking to the SUV. I smile as I realize she is so cold she is snuggling into my side desperately trying to take advantage of my body heat.

Her face against the side of my chest, she whispers. "Thank you, I will not forget this lovely evening."

For some crazy reason, her words have me stopping in my tracks. What in the hell is happening to me? I have made a career of avoiding getting wrangled in by the charms of women. Lifting her chin with my fingers, I lean down, and ever so gently place a soft kiss against her lips, and stare into her eyes. "I too…"

Before I finish the sentence, a blow between my shoulder blades knocks the wind out of me. Jill slips out of my arms, and I watch as she is being whisk away kicking and fighting the ogre restraining her. I lunge forward and take several punches in the gut from a couple of giants on either side of me. Jill is screaming at the ogre, she seems to know him. "Jenkins said he was okay...Damnit, he was just being nice to me. Don't hurt him! Where is Jenkins?"

Doubled over in pain, gasping for air, a slamming hit to my right eye brings me back upright, just in time to get hit with a flying left foot that turns my knees to jelly and my world upside down...The last thing I see is one of them taking a baseball bat to the windows of the ML-63...and my last coherent thought as I hit the sand is...ah damn James is gonna be pissed.

Chapter 4

The next day, a grinding pain situated between my eyes has me waking in a rush of confusion. I attempt to turn, but moan in response to the wrenching pain in my rib cage. I try hard to focus. The entire room is a blur. Soon, I recognize my surroundings and realize I'm in my bed. I clench my jaw and reach into the nightstand drawer and retrieve a pair of glasses. I notice my cell phone, and press the button for James.

James appears immediately. "Boss?"

I grimace. "James, how in the hell did I get home?"

"Well sir, two gentlemen brought you home, handed you over to me with a couple of bottles of pills, and claimed you got yourself into a fight over a woman."

Falling back onto the bed, I groan.

"Boss, I told them that sounded completely out of character, but they didn't seem to want to talk."

I shout. "I was with a woman, true enough. A crazy damn woman, but I was jumped by at least three fat thugs, and another took her from me kicking and screaming." I pause trying to massage my splitting head. "James, what about the ML-63, I'm sure the windows were broken out?"

James raises his eyebrows and says; "Sir, that vehicle was last

36

seen in your possession with all of its windows intact, and is now missing."

Just like I thought, he's pissed. He never calls me sir except when he's pissed.

Flat on my back in bed, I begin my rant. "Who in the hell is that woman? James, I was fuckin' broadsided from behind in the dark."

James takes a step backwards, he had seen me in a lot of situations, but never beaten up like this.

Annoyed I ask. "Tell me James, do I look as bad as I feel?" James shifts his weight from one side to the other, wrinkles his forehead and grinds his answer through his teeth. "I'd say worse. In all these years with you sir, and in observing your constant interaction with ladies; this is the first one to send you home black and blue with stitches. "

I try to roll my eyes at the inference, but the pain in my head and the swelling prevent me from mastering the effect. "Damn, I'm supposed to meet Ruger down in the office; he's in from Santa Fe. By the way, after I finish with Ruger, we will find Jill Maddux. Hell, she might be kidnapped." I murmur.

"Well sir, if I might say so, regardless of this woman's beauty, I think you should stay out of this situation. After all Sir, being beaten and having your vehicle stolen should be warning enough for any man." James steps out, and closes the door.

I push my body up in the bed and begin to mutter to no one. "I knew that woman was trouble. Damn it, just one evening with her and I'm practically killed, and she's missing." Maybe James is right, hell James is always the damn voice of reason. Jill is beautiful, but no, for once James may not realize the entire spectrum of the attraction.

After a quick shower, I at least feel more human and ready to face people.

The look on Diana's face when she spots my bruises makes me want to duck my head. The professional assistant that she is...Diana only winces, before smiling brightly and handing me my messages.

"Miss. Talbert called, Dr. Levine...she is not a happy camper this morning. I did phone her about the cancellation last evening, and I must say she did not take it well. Your other appointments are listed on your notepad."

"Thanks Diana...could you bring me the files and data we received from Ryan, since yesterday...and then get Kim on the phone for me?"

"Yes sir and I will bring you a cup of coffee and a bottle of aspirin as soon as I get those files."

"Thanks."

I pace behind my desk, and attempt to explain. "Kim, I said I was sorry about cancelling our date last night, something came up. Hell, I even apologized about Diana having to call and inform you…Kim; I refuse to respond to rumors. You have no reason to be embarrassed. None of this changes the fact that our outings are not getting either of us anywhere…I'm sorry you thought we had a future…Good luck, Kim." I end the call, relieved, but still confused about what the hell I'm doing.

The inner office line rings, and Diana reminds me. "Dr. Levine, a Brian Goldberg, Ruger, is waiting; in fact he's been out here for quite a while."

"Oh yeah, show him in."

Diana approaches the tall man sitting so patiently. "You can come with me, now. Dr. Levine has finished his conference call."

A soft tap at the door alerts me to the entrance of Ruger. Diana ushers in one of the biggest men I have ever seen! He takes a quick look at my face and smiles slightly; what the hell is he grinning about? Does he think it's funny that I got my ass beat? Just what I need another goon with attitude!

I expect him to say something snarly, and I am ready to knock him down a peg or two. Yet, when he speaks, I am floored.

"How's the kitten?"

"What kitten?" What the hell?

"The one you were trying to save when you fell out of a tree and hit every branch on the way down."

Snapping shut my gaping mouth, I realize this big man has laughing eyes, and I like him! The laugh bursts out of my sore face making me groan and clutch my cheeks. This makes Ruger laugh even harder.

When the pain in my aching face subsides, I answer along the same vein. "The kitten got snatched up by a big gorilla while the other one party danced on my face and kidneys."

Quick as a flash the laughing man before me sobers up and snaps: "Where the hell was your security team?"

"I don't use one in town."

The man could make some really rude noises, and in my own defense I quickly reply;

"Okay, I never used to use one, now I will."

Glancing down at my desk, I see the perfect reminder of why I am now receiving a lecture by a security specialist. Lost in my own thoughts, I gently touch the image and trace her face with one finger.

"I know her. That's Johanna Mueller; she works for the Pentagon doing research analysis. Last time I saw her was in D.C., two years ago. She was working on a magnetic field study that was supposedly cancelled back in the late 70's."

Ruger's voice speaking so close jars me for a moment, then his words hit me like a hammer!

"Johanna Mueller, not Jill Maddux? Are you sure?"

"Hell yes, I never forget a pretty face or a brilliant mind. In her, you get both. Is she using an alias?'

"Apparently so..." This is a turn of events I hadn't expected, I motion Ruger to take a seat across from my desk.

Once he takes a seat, I meet his eyes and in them I see concern. His next question tells me that he is interested in my predicament.

"May not be any of my business, but why don't you tell me what's going on."

Needing to tell someone, I immediately spill everything that has happened since I met Johanna/Jill...whoever she is.

"Are you sure she said 'Jenkins', in the parking lot, and used the words 'Jenkins said he's okay?"

I know Ruger's reputation, and I expect a definitive outlook on the situation, he surprises me again with what I thought was a silly question.

"Yes, that's exactly what she said. Why, does it matter?"
His snort of laughter sets my teeth on edge, and with a quick frown, I let him know he's crossing a boundary, but he raises his hand and I wait for what's coming next.

"Maybe it's just coincidence, maybe not. But, while in

Washington I had the pleasure of working with an Agent Jenkins…Jack Jenkins is an operative with the Federal Witness Protection Program. The feds use the term 'he's okay' when validating someone's presence in the life of a witness."

The hits just keep on coming this morning! "You think Jill…Johanna…damn, what do I call her? Anyway you think she's in the WITSEC Program?"

"First things first, if she's in WITSEC, there's a good possibility she's in deep trouble. Second thing is, if she's protected that deep, then her name is now and forever more…Jill."

"You do not seem awfully concerned by this progression of events. I must say that this is a new experience for me."

"When you have been around as long as I have, nothing much surprises you. I know Johanna, and if she's being protected, then it's because she knows something, not because she did something."

Dad always said, never turn down help when it's standing in front of you, or in this case sitting. "What would you do Ruger, if you were in my shoes?"

"Well three things; number one, I would hire me to ensure your safe. Number two, I would leave her alone…wait…until you know what's going on, and she knows she can trust you. Dig around; a man with your money can buy lots of secrets."

"That's only two, you said three."

"Number three is the biggie; be prepared for the shit to roll downhill. Get out of the way or learn to dodge more often."

"I was expecting you to say forget her."

"No man who has ever met Johanna would forget her. Her presence digs under your skin, and creates a vast need to tuck her under your arm and keep her safe."

"You fall in love with her Ruger?"

I watch Ruger as I ask that question; he smiles softly and shakes his head no. "No man, I had a sister once…long time ago. Johanna always seemed to remind me of what Sherry could have been."

Not sure of how to respond to that remark, I simply pause for a moment.

"Anyway, I guess I should get what I came after, and get on my way."

"Sure Ruger, I have everything ready down in the lab. Just give your keys to my secretary, and she will have the equipment loaded for you. While that's happening, we can step across the street and grab a bite. Maybe, I can pick your brains about a security detail that is unobtrusive and reliable"

"Sounds like a plan."

Rising from my chair, I lead Ruger out into the office area.

With a few words, I direct Diana to have the equipment loaded. Since I have a favorite restaurant just down the block, it doesn't take us long to walk over and take a seat.

My early lunch with Ruger proves to be pleasant experience. After the way my day has started, I am extremely pleased to find that Ruger makes a great distraction. He is funny and has years of experience that make for great stories.

After we finish eating, we walk back together to MLE. Standing in the foyer, I see that something else is on his mind. Gone is the friendly, in place is a more serious man. He hesitates before speaking, I am ready to prompt him, but then he speaks.

"Look, you will most likely think I am crazy, but you can call Brad to confirm what I am about to say. Have you heard about the problems with electrical systems across the country?"

Ah, that is the problem. "Yes, we have installed generators at all of our institutions in case of brown outs and the last few days have seen them used more than ever."

I watch Ruger as he nods, as if agreeing with my preparations. Ruger isn't finished though and I listen carefully as he goes on.

"A group of people I am associated with have come to believe that it will get worse, lots worse, damn soon. In fact, we may be looking at an extended period of darkness that will affect everyone around the world."

44

Just who are these people who are so well informed? "These friends of yours work for NASA?"

"No." Ruger appears to be perplexed as to why I ask that question. "You might say they get their information from alternative sources. Why would you ask that?"

"I have a few friends who work at NASA in Houston, NOAA and the Stennis Space Center down in Mississippi, and all of them have been trying to get the government to listen to their warnings about atmospheric, oceanic, and high altitude changes over the last few months."

"Well, whatever they are seeing is just a portent of what's coming, I am afraid."

"I thought so, that's one of the reasons I had generators installed here in this building, and have made other arrangements to prepare my family."

I think he is going to say more, but it appears as if Ruger has come to the limit of his information.

"I wish I could explain this better. Look, call Brad if he doesn't call you, get him to explain this on a secure line. Be sure to do it soon."

With a quick handshake, I am left standing alone as Ruger rushes out of the building and climbs into a truck.

I walk over to the windows and watch as he drives away. The

glass feels cool as I rest my forehead against it. The scene outside is normal; people hurrying here and there; not a worry in their heads that the sunshine they are enjoying could disappear in a moment, then again why should they?

No matter how they tried, my colleagues and friends across the country could not convince anyone to take them seriously about the coming darkness. Shaking my head at the thoughts that threaten to overpower me…I walk away from the view of all those people I cannot save.

Chapter 5

Sitting in my study, I am processing the information Ruger provided. No wonder she didn't respond when I called out Jill Maddux, her name is Johanna Mueller. I pick up the photograph I took of her at the beach, and gaze. What in the hell is going on with this woman? Without doubt, I know I should cut my losses and forget I ever met her, but can I? I don't accept defeat well.

A knock on the door interrupts my thoughts. "Yes."

James enters. He has that look in his eyes that says Boss you're screwing up, let it go.

"Boss, an Agent Jack Jenkins is here. Perhaps, I should clarify sir, a Federal Agent... I tried to tell him you weren't receiving visitors today, but he says he must speak to you in person, now."

I smirk, and reply in the most sarcastic tone I can muster. "By all means James, send him in; I can't think of anyone I want to see more right now."

James nods, and steps backwards out of the room.

Jack Jenkins enters, obviously surprised by the injuries inflicted upon me by his fellow agents.

"Dr. Levine." Jenkins reaches out to shake my hand. I refuse his gesture and glare at the man standing in front of me. He withdraws his hand, and steps back.

47

In a self-assured tone, he attempts to placate my fury. "Dr. Levine, I understand a terrible series of misunderstandings took place last night. I am here on behalf of the agency to express our most sincere apology."

My laugh startles the Federal agent. "Give me a break Jenkins, and cut the bureaucratic shit. What in the HELL is going on?"

Jenkins clears his throat, and proceeds with his planned explanation. "Well sir, as you might imagine, Jill Maddux's safety is our priority."

My jaw painfully clenched, I hold up my hand in a demand for Jenkins to stop talking. "Just stop right there; I already know the woman is Johanna Mueller."

Unable to mask his surprise, Jenkins responds. "You must be mistaken, her name is Jill Maddux. Surely, Ms. Maddux did not tell you such a ridiculous lie."

I explode. "Jenkins, she did not tell me, I found out from a most reliable source. In fact, right before you got here. Now, you either shoot straight with me or get the fuck out of my sight. You and I both know I could have you and your agent's asses right now, if I wanted."

Jenkins' face turns to fire as he leans over my desk and slams his hand hard against the surface. "You're right, DR. LEVINE, but I trust you will let me get her moved again, before you call on

48

your legal eagles, because you just blew it for her."

I stare hard at Jenkins. "What in the hell do you mean I blew it? When I met that woman she was scared out of her mind. I don't know how you think you prepared her, but you failed miserably. My knowing could only improve her situation, and you damn well know it."

Jenkins straightens his posture and injects. "Policy."

I come back. "Fuck policy."

Jenkins' eyes roll upward as if he is inspecting the ceiling. "What are you suggesting Levine?"

I lean back in my chair, and clasp my hands together in front of me. "I want to know everything."

In a much softer tone, Jenkins asks. "Why?"

I answer in an eerily calm voice. "Because, I don't think you will do your job. You see I don't understand why an agent of your reputation and caliber would have sicced the dogs on me after telling her I was okay. It just doesn't add up."

Jenkins flushes and avoids addressing the later accusation. "You just met her." Jenkins points out.

I nod. "Where is she?"

Jenkins hesitates before answering. "Home."

I look up. "Where's my Mercedes?"

Jenkins replies. "It is being repaired; it will be returned to you by tomorrow."

In a calmer voice, I ask. "What do they want from her, and who are they?"

"I'm speaking the truth; we don't know exactly what they want nor have a lead on the main threat to her; this unsub is truly unknown."

I close my eyes somewhat embarrassed. "Don't move her."

The agent stands for a moment in silence. "Don't you mess with her head, and hurt her. She has suffered enough." With that Jenkins leaves the study.

Again, I pick up the photograph. I mutter. "Johanna Mueller what do you know?"

I stand clenching from the pain ravaging my entire body. Despite the agony, I walk out into the hallway. Outside my high-rise apartment Jenkins is waiting for the elevator.

I demand an answer. "Where in the hell was her security detail?"

Jenkins shakes his head apologetically. "Budgets, we had no reason to believe her relocation or identity was in breach that is until you came along."

I sigh. "Then I will provide it for her."

Jenkins smirks. "If you do that just for her, it will be obvious that you are not only privy to the information, but you shared it.

You see, I would be forced to move her anyway or she will have to give-up our protection, and resume her natural identity."

For a moment, I stand stoic. The elevator opens, and I ask yet another question. "What if she is with me and it's my security?"

Jenkins turns to me with a look of annoyance. "Yeah that would be within reason, but Michael...Dr. Levine, the way I see it is there is still one BIG problem with this so-called solution of yours, and unfortunately, it is one Johanna is totally unaware of at this point. You're a rich son of a bitch, and people, especially people in Texas, care when you take a shit. To top it all off, what happens to her when you're done playing with her and I can't find a place on the planet where she will be safe? She's already lost everything, people, a job she loved and things, all of it gone."

"So why in the hell did you tell her I was safe?"

He chuckles. "I'm an idiot. After she explained the events at the repository, I never believed you would give her a second thought. You see, I just let her enjoy the belief for one day that someone might be interested in her for something, fucking anything, besides classified information."

I glare at him, turn my back on the Federal Agent along with his high opinion of me, and walk away. It's clear to me, Ruger must know what he's talking about; she's even found a spot in the Agent's heart.

Determined to get to the bottom of this mystery and gain some leverage, I dial his cell phone. "Ruger...Michael Levine speaking, hey I know you've got your hands full, but I need some information...I just had a rather heated exchange with Federal Agent Jack Jenkins, there is something about him and the situation with Johanna that just rubs me the wrong way...this isn't funny Ruger!

Don't you have any dirt I can use on the man ... Nobodies that clean ...Oh, White House Security ... huh? Well can you check his team, there's something going on Ruger, I tell you I can feel it! Thanks, I owe you one...ok maybe two. Stop laughing at me Ruger! I am not strung out over her!

Are you guys prepared out there?...Yeah, just wait and see for now...Give me your HAM Radio freq and call sign before you hang up. Yeah mine is M1LEC, I stay up around 420 MHz, but can go up or down if needed.

Take care Ruger, and don't forget the dirt!"

Chapter 6

A clear night, I stare out over the city's skyline as it falls off into to the dark abyss of the hidden ocean. The view from my office is magnificent by anyone's standards. No time to gaze, I turn back to face the cad drawings on my monitor. It's late, and I want to send them to prototype tomorrow. The new adjustments to the ground penetrating radar are cutting-edge. A similar comparison would be the difference between an old tin-type and digital high-definition photo. It will surely drown out any meager competition and gain MLE the remaining shares of the market. I am concentrating on the perimeters, a tedious task I have already repeated several times, but one small mistake could delay the project's release by months.

Suddenly, as I'm finishing my final review, everything except my monitor goes black. I look towards the windows and gasp. The entire city is black. I pick up my cell phone to contact NOAA, its dead. I reach for the land line, nothing. The warnings over the last few days rebound inside my head, my mouth goes dry, there's little doubt about what is happening, in all likelihood come morning the sun will not appear.

My thoughts are interrupted by a tap on the door. "Yes?" James enters carrying several flashlights. "Boss, the generators should be up and running in a moment, but until then here's a

couple of flashlights, the power company should get right on this."
I accept the flashlights. "James, this has me a bit concerned, my
cell won't work either, it is more probable than not science's worst
nightmare is manifesting within this very moment; this is not a
simple grid failure." I see through the glow of the flashlight the
fear shadowing James' face. A concern I cannot resolve at the
moment. "James, are all of the vehicles fully gassed up?

James answers quickly. "I believe so, sir."

"If the power returns, you make sure all of them are sitting with
full tanks and you keep it that way until further notice, be sure the
extra tanks on the SUV are also topped off."

"Absolutely, Boss. Umm, I'm going to go check with
maintenance to see what's holding up the generators?" I nod.
James follows the shimmering light to exit.

Operating on stored energy, the monitor with drawings for the
prototype shines back at me. I save my work and shut the program
down. Sitting in the dark room with the faded glow of the rather
small flashlight James brought me, I begin to speculate in my mind
about the current circumstance. All estimations suggested the
darkness could last from seventy-two to eighty hours. In the crux
of my thoughts, an image of the woman flashes through my mind.
In a state of urgency, I deduct, Johanna/Jill, whatever, couldn't
possibly be equipped to handle even the slightest emergency. She

didn't even have a glass to drink from in her cabinets.

The lights flicker back on; I gasp a sigh of relief, the generators are operating. I head to the stairwell leading to my apartment. Inside my personal study, I unlock the cabinet, and remove three handguns, all of which I have Concealed Carry Permits. My favorites are the HK45, the smaller Glock 23 and the Kahr PM9. I had all three fitted with the threaded barrel option which allows for the use of suppressors. After checking the ammunition, I grab a few magazines, and lock it back.

"Boss?" James questions from behind. I turn and hand one of the guns to him.

"Boss you know I don't like guns and abhor violence."

"Yeah well, you shouldn't have become a personal bodyguard then!"

"You know I am a perfectly good defensive driver, and my close combat skills are beyond reproach! Besides, I make the best omelets', iron the crispest shirts and keep the cleanest house within a thousand miles." James responds defensively.

"Yes, but your resume states, and the reason my father hired you all those years ago, was because you are a bodyguard."

"Perhaps sir, but that's your body I am guarding not someone else's, and if I may so sir, you are the one who put yourself in harm's way when you went out alone with that strange woman..."

"We have to go get her James."

"I knew you were going to say that."

"James, stop being such a ninny and help me get this vest on."

"Boss, that woman got the hell beat out of you? Yes, and did you forget about the Federal Agent knocking at your door?"

I smirk, careful not to reveal her real name to James. "Yes James, her, Jill Maddux, now come on, and no I did not forget about the agent. Like hell, if I'm going to let him get to her before I do. Grab some flashlights and I'll meet you in the garage. We'll take the Suburban; it's a tank, besides we'll need to bring some of her clothes and things."

"What about that Agent?" I cut James off. "Don't worry James; if Jack Jenkins can't find her, I'm the first person he'll come looking for…"

"Precisely my point sir," James laughs; clearly my sudden concern about this woman and the idea would demand a good chuckle. Of course, if she didn't have trouble written all over her footprints, and it wasn't the night the lights went out in Corpus Christi.

Sitting tensely in the front seat, I keep an expectant eye out for trouble. With the blackout, the street lights and signal lights are all out. Police stand on every corner directing traffic, and the snarl of anxious drivers permeates the air.

With the windows down, I can hear the voices of those standing around near the streets...

"You think it's another terrorist attack?"

"Maybe someone blew up the power plant?"

"I think we would have noticed the explosion."

"My cell phones not working...why would the blackout knock out all the cell towers? I thought they had some sort of backup systems?

I want to lean my head out the window and yell at them; "Get your dumb asses off the streets and prepare your families for chaos!" But I can't do anything, but watch anxiously as James guides the Suburban along the dark and crowded streets.

Finally, I breathe a sigh of relief as we turn off on the narrow street fronting Johanna's house.

James stands watch near the Suburban.

With my flashlight I inspect the property, make way through the pitch black, and knock hard against Johanna's darkened front door. No answer the third time, I yell. "It's me Michael...Michael Levine, I want to help you." Something innate tells me she's in there scared out of her mind. I hesitate, not wanting to further traumatize her, but I can't think of another reasonable option. "STAND BACK, I'M COMING IN!" I pull the Glock out, take a deep breath, aim and shoot into the door lock. The door jars, and

I rush inside.

Scanning each room on the lower level with the aid of my flashlight, I notice, despite her failure to yet purchase customary basics, she has a fully furnished and functional office. In a hurry, my peaked curiosity will have to wait, I must find Johanna.

Upstairs, I glance into two empty bedrooms; in a third, I find a studio. I pause, just as she claimed, she really does paint, and she does it with real talent. I step back in the hall, shine the light to the closed door at the end, and assume this is the master bedroom where she sleeps.

I take gentle steps to the door, turn the knob, and open. Quietly, I enter another well-furnished room and find Johanna sitting perched in the center of her bed, talking, but not to me. I place the Glock back into the harness as I stare silently at her. What the hell is she saying? Better yet, who in the hell is she saying it to?

An octave above a whisper, I call out her name. "Johanna, it's me, Michael."

She replies, but not to me. "Please, tell me why it works, I simply must understand."

I'm standing in front of her bed, stoic. After a short while, I speak again. "Johanna you're dreaming, please wake up."

"Michael, you're here too? Where are we?"

58

I gasp. "We are in your bedroom."

"Michael, I can hear you, but I can't see you and this is not my bedroom."

I move closer to her, reach out and touch her hand. "Johanna, I can see you, we are in your bedroom."

Her body suddenly jerks, startling me. She looks bewildered.

"Michael why are you here? Are you really here?"

I sit on the edge of the bed next to her. "Yes, I'm really here. I'm here to take you with me."

Bemused she asks. "Why? Where did the others go?"

"Johanna, you were dreaming."

She shakes her head. "No, it wasn't a dream. You must believe me. It was strange, but it wasn't a dream. " Tears begin rolling down her cheeks. She moves to me and I wrap my arms around her. She whispers. "Did you call me Johanna?"

"Yes."

"Oh no!"

I hush her, and stroke her hair. "It's okay, Jenkins knows, I'll explain later. Listen to me, we need to gather your things, with this blackout, it is not safe here for you."

She tilts her head up. "What blackout?" Her eyes widen before I can answer, and she screeches. "Oh my God, what did they do to you?"

I pull her in tighter. "Shhh, I'm fine, but we really need to gather your things. James, my driver, is waiting to help us. We can talk when we get to my place. I have generators and everything we need to ride out this disaster."

"Driver?"

"Yes, come on now."

"What do you mean blackout?"

"Electricity and communications have gone black over the entire city and I suspect beyond, and we are most likely looking at days without light of any form...not even sunlight or moonshine; but at this point I am not sure of anything."

I rise, grasping her hand, and gently tug helping her out of the soft bed. In the glow of the flashlight, I look at her not so revealing white cotton gown and smile.

Her feet firmly planted on the floor, she freezes. "Oh no, it's for real? What about Jenkins, he will surely send someone for me."

I face her, and smile hoping she can see. "He will eventually send someone, but he will know to check my place. Your man Jenkins and I had a bit of an exchange the other day."

I can see her puzzled look, but her next thought is more puzzling. "I hope Jenkins is okay, and what about Monica, the baby is due in less than a month?"

I roll my eyes knowing full well she cannot see. "Dare I ask who Monica is?"

Johanna giggles. "Monica is his darling wife; they are sort of my family, now."

This explains a whole lot. "Really, well I am quite sure Jack Jenkins has the where with all to take care of his wife and unborn baby. Right now, I intend to get your stuff and get you in a safer place."

Again she smiles. "I don't really know you very well."

I chuckle. "Right now lady, I'm the best you got, just help me get your clothes and anything else you don't want looters to pilfer."

Finally, the conversation ceases and we begin rushing through the bedroom stuffing belongings into suitcases and bags. Soon, I am satisfied that we have retrieved enough of Johanna's clothes, toiletries and personal belongings from her room.

Moving to the front door I yell at James. "James, grab as much of her painting supplies and art from the studio as we can fit."

James responds. "Got it Boss."

"Michael, I should change."

I look down and then up her body, and throw her a pair of sneakers. "I wouldn't worry about anyone seeing too much of you in that, just put your shoes on." She looks at me, but quietly complies.

Her hand in mine, I hurriedly rush her downstairs and move

her into the office. Sarcastically, I tease as I inspect the room with my flashlight. "At least I understand where your priorities rest. An office and bedroom before eating utensils, even I am not that committed to work." She gives me a soft equally sarcastic smile.

I begin hauling out piles of notebooks, files and a laptop. I wonder why she does not take advantage of the digital world; surely, the FBI keeps her electronics safe.

Soon forced, I admit defeat. "We are all out of room Jill, I'm sorry at this stage anymore, and you'll be riding on my lap." Her eyes confirm she realizes I called her Jill in front of James for good reason.

Again, her eyes are saying something, and I ask James to return to the Suburban. "What is it?"

She leads me to the kitchen, and removes a very large flathead screwdriver, hands it to me and leads me back to the office. Inside, she shuts the door and points down to the wooden planks on the floor. I look at her. "What do you want me to do?"

She clears her throat. "Remove the plank; I really need to take the box."

I stare at her, before kneeling down. Carefully, I slide the flat edge into the slight groove and pop the piece of flooring with attached sub-flooring out of its space. Beneath I find a narrow file box, and remove it. I glance up at Johanna and she nods. I replace the piece and together with the box in hand we proceed to the front door.

Johanna begins to shut the door, and pauses. I look down at her and laugh. "Sorry, you wouldn't answer. Close it and we'll hope no one comes to open it"

We rush to the Suburban, I open the door to the backseat for Johanna, seated, I hand her the seat belt; she buckles and takes the file box from me, protectively holding it in her lap. My eyes widen as I wonder what the box contains, but quickly I come to my senses and close the door.

I walk around to the back of the Suburban to check the doors. Suddenly, I freeze and slowly raise my hands behind my head. The spotlight is so close to my back I can feel the heat radiating.

In a raised voice of sarcasm I say. "Jenkins?"

"Levine?"

I address Jenkins from a sardonic tone. "Yeah, no surprise, I beat your ass here."

Jenkins orders his fellow agents. "Relax." He approaches my back, shoves my arms down, and probes. "Gotta a permit for that piece Dr. Levine?"

"I sure as hell do and so does my driver…happy to show you."

Jenkins ignores the offer, and glances into the back of the SUV. "What is up with all this stuff?"

My shoulders relax as I turn to face Jenkins. "You're forgetting that I'm a scientist, chances are this darkness isn't going to rescind anytime soon, and if I'm right nothing will be the same again anyway. If estimations are correct the sun will remain obscured for three days. I'm guessing you can't even get D.C. right now, better find yourself some HAM radios, because the government did not listen to guys like me, and outside of the Oval Office, they've done nothing."

Eyebrows raised, Jenkins changes the subject back to matters at hand. "So you're taking her with you? Why?"

Surely, Jenkins doesn't think I'm going to start confiding in him. Besides, I am beginning to wonder if he is aware of the science that seems to be consuming Johanna's attention, perhaps the agent is not quite on the right path. "It's just as I told you, I think I'll do your job better than you. Why don't you just go home and take care of your wife and blossoming family."
Jenkins glares. "Where the hell did you get that information?"

I grin and impose an annoyingly long pause. "Don't you think you crossed the professional line with your charge? How would the agency feel about that? She's more worried about your unborn baby than you are."

Jenkins cocks his head back with a contorted look on his face.

"I need to talk to her; she needs to tell me she wants to go with you."

I wave my hand in a gesture. "Go ask her, I'll wait right here Special Agent Jack Jenkins."

After several moments, Jenkins returns to face me waiting for him behind the Suburban. I smirk. "Where were you going to take her, home with you?"

Jenkins kicks at the driveway with his boot. "It doesn't really matter now, does it? But, your ego can take a hike Levine and understand, I am a married man, I don't feel that way about Jill."

I raise my eyebrows. "I didn't think it was THAT…Something tells me, the agency would think making her family as in the baby's pseudo aunt is inappropriate, unethical and could put her in danger. I'm not completely sure yet, but because she is so fond of you, your wife, and unborn child, she probably doesn't bother you to meet her own needs." I end with a sadistic smile.

Jenkins rubs his chin. "Okay Levine, what the hell is it you want?"

"Carte Blanche, Oh, and an escort back to my place."

He stares at me. "Get in the fucking truck, we'll follow you, and I will talk to her when we get to your place."

I smile big; "My pleasure."

Chapter 7

When our small convoy reaches the park near MLE, we stop. A small crowd of people are just standing in the road. Inside our vehicles we sit and watch for a moment as we spot what has caught the crowds' attention.

The darkness seems to lift briefly, and then the ground appears to shimmer for a moment. I set spellbound as I watch what appears to be shadows separate from the ground and undulate in wide strips moving towards the crowd.

Panic sets in immediately, and people run screaming from the shadows. I step out of the suburban, and stand calmly as the strips move towards me.

"Get back in the vehicle you fool!" Jenkins yells.

"No, it's okay, they are Shadow Bands, rare but fully explainable. It's a side effect of the current atmospheric anomalies."

"Why are people running away then?" Jenkins asks as he joins me.

"What the eyes see, and the mind knows, and what the body will accept as normal does not allow most people to stand still when the ground starts crawling towards them. This is just the beginning, and we will see more and more strange occurrences."

"Well, let's get on the way. I have other worries." Jenkins snaps as he nervously tries to step over a shadow band and re-enter the vehicle.

We continue our drive back to MLE and spot several more shadow bands before the darkness falls once more.

After Jenkins speaks to Johanna in the MLE parking garage, I lead her to the elevator, and we ride up to my apartment on the thirtieth floor. Once inside, Johanna's eyes move around the massive modern space. The bold earth tones seem to appeal to her.

"I guess you really are quite the businessman Dr. Levine."
I give her a soft smile. "James will put your personal belongings in the guest room closest to mine. As for the rest, I will direct him to a suitable arrangement."

She whispers. "Thank you."

Again her eyes dance around the room. "This situation is bad isn't it Dr. Levine?"

I stare wondering why she continues to call me Dr. Levine.

"Michael…Yes, tomorrow Johanna we may not see the sun rise and I believe the darkness is a disaster outweighing all previous known to man."

She looks down. "Why am I here?"

"You certainly had a choice. Jenkins gave you the opportunity to go with him so, why are you here?" I am certainly not ready to answer any profound questions.

Her head raises and her posture becomes straighter as if I slapped her. "Truthfully, I don't know." Her tone is strong with a hint of anger.

"Oh, I think you do." She shrugs and refuses to comment.

Knowing I am crossing a line, I continue. "You don't trust Jenkins. I'm not sure whether your distrust is based on the event at the beach the other night or previous situations."

The blood rushes to Johanna's face and her tone imamates. "How dare you say such a despicable thing? I did not ask for your help."

I rub my face with my hands. "You did ask, maybe not in words, but... Let me clarify; you don't trust Jenkins when it's important."

"Oh and I trust you?" Exasperated, she shouts.

My forehead wrinkles. "You're hoping."

James appears providing a much needed interruption. "Sir, Ms. Maddux's personal things are in the guest room, everything is prepared for her if she would like to retire." I pick up on the hint of sarcasm in James' voice.

I thank and dismiss him. "I'll show you to your room, unless you would like something to eat or drink." My tone is curt.

"No thank you, I will be fine."

I roll my eyes at her little pun and lead her to the room. "I believe everything is here, but if you need anything, I'm in the next room." She nods and I leave shutting the door behind me.

After making arrangements with James in regards to the rest of Johanna's things, I pour a Brandy and retreat to my bedroom. I look around at the black, grey, and white surrounding me and wonder if it needs a splash of color. Johanna, she is a touch of color in my sterile world. I admonish myself, how can I be thinking of romance and decorating with the threat of impending epic disaster looming over everything?

I take out my Blackberry and once more attempt to call NOAA, again, nothing. I think of my aging parents, two brothers, sister and their families. Although they are well educated and prepared for the disaster, if I can't reach them by phone, I will need to make contact with them tomorrow.

I remove my shoes and shirt before setting on the bed. It feels good to stretch my legs out in comfort on the large platform bed. I take a sip of Brandy savoring the pleasant burn in my throat. With closed eyes I curve my head back. Now sorry, I handled Johanna too harshly, my words have left me unable to ask her about anything tonight.

A little more relaxed, now I open my laptop and begin

reviewing the atmospheric event and the possible cyclical contributors.

I search for a paper in which I was initially introduced to the theory of DMT and its symptoms, like the effects of lack of sunlight on the body during a cosmic event. Johanna explained her experience was not like a dream. She seemed to allude to the fact that it was interactive. Like a light bulb turning on, I realize until the days of darkness pass this experience will plague us, and we might not be able to sleep, or more likely; should not sleep deeply. The different hormones the body produces in direct proportion to light received are all psychotropic. That means the over-production of those produced during dark hours versus the decrease of those produced during daylight will play hell with human emotions and the ability to reason properly.

I ponder as I think about Johanna; she did not seem horrified as the theorists had warned. I close my computer and rush to the guest room where she might very well be falling asleep.
I crack open the door, and sure enough, I hear her speaking. She sounds annoyed and frustrated, but not afraid. I rush to my study and grab a voice recorder and a notepad.

I reenter the room. She is setting up in the bed having a conversation with someone and I sure as hell can't see them. I jot, noting everything I see.

I watch her as she begins speaking about elements. The way she uses her hands in gestures is perplexing. After a few moments, the tone seems to change and she begins to show signs of irritation. I contemplate and wonder if it is time for me to intervene. I study her closely.

She begins speaking loudly. "I don't understand."

I watch her pause as if she is listening intently to a normal conversation. Yet, she draws together her brows in tension.

"Why must you be so vague? I want to understand, but you must speak up. I practiced the sign language like I promised, and I speak slowly and clearly like you taught me. Why won't she answer?"

I surmise Johanna is apparently attempting to communicate with a deaf person in her dream!

"I tried to stop them Cindy, you must believe me! What more could I have done besides die with you? No, please don't be angry…don't leave! I have the work… it is safe, and I will never let them find it." I cringe just listening to her plead with these people.

"Adam, please try to make her understand. Yes I hid, but only after there was no more hope of helping the two of you. I stayed and I listened to you both die…never will I forget that. You were both so brave and you saved me…don't regret that moment, I will not let you down. I promise…"

71

Silent tears are running down her cheeks, and her voice sounds as if she is reliving some horrible moment. It's too much, I rush to her side. "Johanna, come back."

Unlike before, she comes back to reality immediately.

"Michael?"

"I'm right here."

"I went there again. It's the atmosphere isn't it?"

Stunned, I whisper; "I did some referencing, and yes, I think so. Are you familiar with the alleged reasons behind the phenomenon, Johanna?

"A little…in one sense it's awesome, even so, it's also somewhat frightening. Did you go there too?"

I shake my head. "No, I haven't fallen asleep yet."

"I'm not sure I want to fall asleep again, at least for a while."

I hear my Blackberry ringing in the next room, and rush to answer it.

"Ryan! Glad you got through…yes; it's started here as well. No…I haven't heard from anyone else. I know you're scared, but you're safe inside the facility… If nothing else, bar yourself and one other person you trust in a single room, and do not sleep and do not come out until this is over…No, no sleep, if you sleep you will enter a state of paranoia and delusions…I can't get there right now, I would if I could…Who can you trust?…No not him!…Look, go find Mary Charters, the two of you get inside my office, barricade the doors, and stay there....Ryan, Ryan!...Calm down, do what I tell you, try to send me any updates you can before the power fails again....Listen to me, inside my office is a door with a keypad lock, the combination is 1411, open that door, there is a small area set up with a generator, food, and supplies. Stay there until you hear from me or from someone who uses the phrase...um...bright and shiny...

I have to go now, I need to call my family...Go get Mary, get inside my office and then call those you need to. Stay safe Ryan. I return to the room to sit with Johanna, but continue with my calls. Unsure, of how long the service will remain, I take full advantage of the reprieve.

I hang up, satisfied that I spoke to everyone that matters at the moment; I glance over at a very patient, but expectant Johanna. I know she wants information, but I'm not sure how much I want to share.

The sun should be climbing up now to greet the morning, but for the first time the entire human race must face a morning of complete darkness. This is the hour in which all will soon realize what scientists all over the world spent the night trying to stomach.

For thousands of years we have worked to not only rid

ourselves from the boundaries of nature but to rise above it. We believed we had outrun nature's powers. We have lived by the light of day and blotted out the night…wrested our fear of the dark, with the absence of a single sunrise, all the gifts of Prometheus and the talismans of hope have faded.

I see the tension rising in Johanna as she stares hopelessly out the massive window. I long to comfort her and the thought makes me feel uncomfortable. I shake my head and rub my rough unshaven face with my hands. I should be in Miami at NOAA. Why did I bring this woman here in the midst of a disaster knowing I should instead be making my way to my other home in Miami? The Agency needs me and I need the Agency, but Johanna Mueller needs me too.

What can I do with her? It is exasperating. I sure as hell am not going to call Jenkins and say sorry NOAA needs me, I was just kidding. She seems like a feminine woman, well put together in an east coast city way, a heels and dresses woman, not a rugged woman.

The woman must be reading my mind. "Dr. Levine they need you. You must go."

Unnerved, I look at her expressionless. "What are you talking about?"

She speaks in an honest tone. "At Julio's you said you work in the field when it interests you. It is hard to imagine this situation would not intrigue you. Jenkins will make sure I'm safe."

Just hearing the man's name puts me on edge. "Well Miss Mueller for your information, I have a family here in Corpus that matters to me." I sure as hell am not going to admit she intrigues me every bit as much as the days of darkness. I will just try to figure out how I can feed the need for both.

Johanna flushes. "I'm so sorry. I don't know why, but it did not occur to me that you might have children."

I shake my head. "I don't have children, but I do still have parents and siblings."

Her eyes grow huge. "Oh."

I stand and walk towards the door. She calls out to me. "Is it okay if I shower?"

I pause, "Of course."

Entering my bedroom, I open the closet and reach up for the box that lies on the top shelf. Taking it to the bed I dump its contents and rifle through them. Pausing at the photograph of my family taken on the shores of Galveston, it was a good day, a bright and shiny day. My tired mind loses focus as I remember the laughter and the sounds of the waves, and the feel of the sunshine....

An eerie thick fog surrounds me, grotesque shadows are lurking everywhere. I hear her voice at the end of the strange tunnel of darkness. "Dr. Levine...Michael...Michael come back."

I return to find my body is drenched in sweat, and Johanna's face next to mine. I throw my arms around her and envelope her in a tight embrace. She squeezes the words from inside my tight grip. "You fell asleep and went there."

I breathe hard remembering the horrifying experience. My hands begin moving up and down her back in an attempt to reassure myself that she is real and in my own time and space. Her freshly washed hair tickles my nostrils, and I breathe a sigh of relief.

"Michael, please say something." She's begging, but I don't say a word. My hands move to grasp her face and I stare deep into her beautiful dark eyes. I glare hard in wonder until my lips press hard against hers in a rough kiss. Her body tightens, I don't know if she wants to because she can't respond. I continue for several long moments.

She squeals bringing me back from my trance. I shout. "James." Setting Johanna to the side, I leap off the bed to find James. I rush down the outer hallways, and then pound on the door of his studio. After several long moments, he opens the door looking bewildered and soaking wet.

"James you can't go to sleep. Do you hear me? Until the days of darkness pass you must stay awake. Sleep is now a horrifying hallucinogen."

Still in a state of shock, he nods, and I turn and walk away. Inside the apartment, I find Johanna setting on the curvy sofa with her hands clasp in her lap. I say nothing as I make my way to the kitchen where I press the button on the coffeemaker. James prepared it last night. Coffee mugs in place I call out to her in the other room. "Cream…Sugar?"

Void of emotion she answers. "Just cream."

I approach her with two cups of coffee and hand her one. "I'll be showering now." She looks at me, but doesn't respond.

Carrying my coffee, I turn on the shower, and allow the water to heat. As I undress, I wonder just how in hell we are supposed to survive the coming days; high on caffeine and running from our own minds.

As I drop my clothes in the hamper, I give an involuntary shudder as a brief image of the hallucination, dream, nightmare…whatever the hell it was comes crashing back.

Grabbing my coffee, I take it with me into the shower. With my back to the hot water, I drink my coffee; trying to relax my muscles while at the same time revving up my adrenaline levels.

Talking to myself is a habit from childhood, and I still use it.

"I would beat my head against this wall if I thought it would erase the memories."

"Yeah, but then all you would have is a concussion, and that could put you to sleep. Not too smart are you?"

"Smart enough…then again, maybe not." I sigh loudly.

"Oh yeah… if you are so smart, then why aren't you in Miami making sure Larson Taylor isn't screwing the world over in order to make himself famous?"

"He wouldn't do that!"

"The hell he wouldn't! He could have released that data nine months ago. NO, he held onto it, why? Because he didn't want to rock any politicians' boats; it's an election year, you know?"

"No one would listen then any more than they have in the past few weeks. Ryan and the others have taken it all the way to the Hill, and no one would give them even a minute second thought."

"Bet they are running around now looking for 'experts' and talking heads!"

"Probably so, but it's too late for them, for us, for the rest of the world."

"Your depressing you know?"

"So go find somebody else to talk too."

"I will, as soon as I finish my coffee."

"Well make it snappy, my ass is getting cold in here!"

I emerge from the Master Suite to find Johanna still stoic and planted firmly on the sofa.

 words sting; "You are a cranky man that likes to control everything. No wonder your journey to the other side was so ugly."

My head doesn't move, but my eyes roll to the side. "That is no revelation Miss Mueller. In fact, isn't that exactly why you're here?"

Her lips pressed together hard, she shrugs. "Hmm!"

My eyes roll mocking her behavior. "Well, at least we understand one another."

"You do not understand me Dr. Levine."

I smirk. "Oh but I do, remember I'm a control freak. Control freaks are constantly aware; they miss nothing, my dear lady. Jenkins doesn't have a clue about you, does he? In fact, you have work unrelated to your job at the Pentagon, right?"

"You must still be hallucinating because I don't know what you are talking about."

I further fuel her fire by answering her in a sardonic tone. "I guess I was wrong then." I smile.

Surprising the hell out of me, she calls out as I move to leave the room. "Just in case, you and your controlling state of madness

79

are compelled to know, you're right about one thing and only one, I don't mind that you are a CRANKY CONTROL FREAK. In fact to the contrary, I like it."

I stop dead, unsure how to respond; I pivot and stare blankly at the woman seated on my sofa. Living in constant danger, of course she likes it. She really isn't like the others. Strong in her own right, she isn't trying to prove anything to me.

Now, what to say? I'll just do what I always do when things get a little emotional, ask an unrelated question. "Johanna, when you're not in hiding, what do you do?"

Confused, she looks at me from a contorted face. "I thought you knew I am or rather was a research specialist. By the way, you didn't bother to tell me how you found out."

I laugh this isn't the answer I need, but I'll respond to it anyway. "I do know you were a research specialist, I wanted to know what you do when you are not working or hiding. Nevertheless, I met with an old friend of yours the other day about a completely unrelated matter, but he told me plenty."

Now, I have her attention. "Who?"

"Brian Goldberg; better known as Ruger."

Her face lights up and I don't know how I feel about her reaction. "Oh wow! How is he? What is Ruger doing? What on earth did he tell you about me? Ruger and I were the best of friends during his time at the Pentagon."

I flush at the thought of her and Ruger being so close, but I explain without revealing my jealousy or at least I think I do. "Ruger is working for an anthropologist, Antonio Dominguez. Antonio is the one that recently found King Solomon's Scrolls, apparently keeping him and the rather odd as Ruger put it, Amanda Messenger, Antonio's girlfriend and partner safe is a big job in recent weeks."

"As for you, the feelings are mutual; he spoke very highly of you and is quite concerned about your well-being. He is responsible for assembling a security detail for me, scheduled to begin next week. Of course all of this was arranged prior to the onset of darkness."

She squints at me.

"Johanna, you have yet to answer my original question."

She smiles at me. "Perhaps, you could make yourself a little clearer, sir. I do lots of things, do I need a resume?"

I can't help, but chuckle. "I would like to know what kind of activities you have participated in in the past."

She looks perturbed. "I am very durable, what do you need me to do?"

"Answer the question."

"I like to swim, bike, and I love whitewater rafting. Oh and I do

81

Pilates. Is that good enough sir?"

I shake my head and answer. "Yes, it is more than acceptable."

"Good, now why?"

"I'm not sure yet, but I will be sure to tell you if it comes to fruition."

She lets out an exasperated sigh. "Fine."

I've been around long enough to know, when a woman says fine hell is about to break loose.

Chapter 8

Johanna Mueller

The soft glow from the MLE building's security lights are my only guide as I step out. Michael will be furious, but I must see this for myself in order to understand. There is a continuous sound of sirens, it is unnerving. People are pouring into the street. Many appear to have stepped out of a zombie movie. They don't have a clue about the situation at hand. Without consistent news reports the details must be sketchy for most people. Their ignorance of this event will prove to be their worst demise.

Creeping down the sidewalk surrounding Michael Levine Enterprises, I realize even in the midst of the charcoal grayness of the lights, it is a massive building. Whatever he really does, it is most impressive and successful. As an ambulance screams past, I have to cover my ears...the sound is too loud in the otherwise strange quiet.

The air is heavy now, and it is sort of uncomfortable to breathe. Where is the breeze? This close to the Gulf the reality of the lack of air movement is incomprehensible; I'll ask Michael about this element of the phenomenon.

Stopping on the corner in front of the building, I watch in awe as all those around me are panicking, many are talking to themselves, others are crying out to God, but no one seems to notice me, it's as if I am invisible. I'm simply observing the chaotic mayhem unfolding.

Parents grip their children's hands and carry small bags as they attempt to get someplace where they will feel safer; a parent's house, a police station, a shelter. Their mindsets are stuck in normal reactions to emergencies; when there is a hurricane, seek shelter further inland, the authority figures will have the answer, just find them, Mom and Dad will know what to do.

Others wander aimlessly taking in the new darkness as if they are observing momentary phenomena. Walking and pausing they look up at the sky seeking signs of coming morning.

Looters and those who prey on the weak are running rampant, breaking windows, snatching bags from weaker people. A few policemen are trying to help, telling people to return home…their voices are not the self-assured timbres they usually have, and the people sense their weakness.

Turning to my left, I see a woman just sitting on the curb, holding a baby and crying as she rocks it. Her voice carries to me..."He'll be back darling. Daddy wouldn't leave us in this. I'm sure he didn't mean what he said. Mommy will keep you safe; just give me a moment to figure out how."

So it begins, the frail and the weak abandoned, the strong taking what they want, and the rest will be left to deal with the consequences.

Michael Levine

The morning of the first day of darkness and chaos is already gripping Earth's inhabitants. On the ground floor of Michael Levine Enterprises, I am staring out at the street in front of the building. The people are shadows walking around aimlessly, it's chilling. Some are screaming or crying while others meander around in shock. I am peering out at the back of a woman who appears to be studying the anguish. A deviant looking man with outstretched hands is approaching her from behind, and she doesn't see him. My God it's Johanna!

I am racing over to the door and stopped by one of my building security guards. "Dr. Levine, sir, you do not want to go out there. Horrible things are happening."

Furious, I am spitting out orders. "Bob, let me out. See that woman; she's with me. I'm going to grab her and you need to let us back in." Bob is nodding with huge eyes, as he unlocks and opens the door quickly to let me out.

My adrenal is pumping, as I run out. Picking Johanna up, I throw her over my shoulder. She yells. "Michael, let me down." I ignore her as we race through the door. In a fit of rage, I carry her through the ground floor office and into a boardroom in the back of the building. I kick slam the door shut, and finally, I set Johanna down on the floor.

I feel red with rage, and my dark eyes are livid. "WHAT IN HELL WERE YOU DOING OUT THERE? Seriously, are you certifiably crazy? Anything could happen to you in the streets." Standing, she stares at me as my arms flail in a rant. "Damn you Johanna." I continue to yell, but instead of backing off, she is moving in closer.

In a whisper, she asks. "Are we all going to die?"

Briefly, behind closed eyes, I take a deep breath. "Not all of us."

She moves closer until her head is resting against my chest. My arms in the air, I glance up at the ceiling.

"I'm sorry, I just had to see it, hear the sounds, and smell the smells. I needed to feel something besides my own fear. I want to do something for them, but what?"

I reach down, and wrap my arms around her pulling her further into my chest. "It's too late for many of them. There is nothing any of us can do, unless they prepared not even a scientist can help, now. There are too many, I am struggling with that myself. I feel the need to find a way to travel to NOAA and help the team, but in reality there is not a damn thing we can do. In the past, our warnings were often curtailed, quieted, and ignored, this is the price."

"Please, there is a young woman sitting out there with a baby, surely we can do something for them?"

As much as I want to say no…I know I am going to say yes.

"Where did you see her?"

Johanna is running back to the front of the building as I follow closely. She searches frantically and finally sees her.

"There beside the pillar, see them?"

"Bob open the door once more, and then, if I ask again you can shoot me."

"Okay sir, but just remember you said that."

As the door opens a crack, I rush over to the young woman.

Kneeling down beside her, I speak softly.

"Miss, come inside with me, bring your baby and I will find a place for you to be safe and if you want get you to your family as soon as I can."

She looks up at me with dazed eyes and for a moment I think

she is too far gone. Then a flicker of hope flashes in the depths.

"Really? We won't be much bother! I have everything she needs right here in this bag. I don't need food or anything, just help me keep her safe!"

I help her to her feet and take the bag she has guarded so well by sitting on it. "Come on, let's get off the street." Even as I speak, shots are ringing out, car windows shattering and people are beginning to run in real panic.

I'm pulling the woman close to my body, hunched over her small frame I run to the door where Bob swings it open and uses one beefy hand to yank us inside.

"Drop the shutters, Hal!" I yell to the guard sitting behind the control desk.

The immediate sound of metal scraping against brick is making a resounding noise in the lobby. The thick hurricane shutters slam down with a vengeance and the instantaneous quiet of suppressed sounds from outside is heavenly.

Now locked in, I walk over to the desk, and with a quick glance make sure all of the shutters are down on all entrances. I then reach over and pull out the key that activates the release. I put the key in my pocket, and with a glance make sure everyone understands what that means; no one will be leaving or entering without my permission or until I put the key back.

"Did all of you bring your families in like I said?" I ask.

"Yes sir, we took over those empty apartments on the third floor like you said. There are me, Bob, Alvin, and Jerry and our families up there. I'm sorry to say that two of the younger men decided to leave and not come back." Hal answers.

"I'm sorry too…This young lady and her baby will need a place to stay, any ideas where she could fit in?"

Bob clears his throat. "Sir if she wants, she can stay with me and my Mama, we got plenty of room in that big old apartment up there. Mama would like the company, and she's good with babies."

Turning to the young mother, I smile.

"You can trust Bob, and his Mama, they are good people, and you will both be taken care of."

Walking over to the giant of a man, she holds out her free hand, in a voice made firm by desperation and hope, she speaks.

"My name is Leigh, and this is Haley, better known as Monkey. We appreciate your offer and would be glad to join you. I can help with the cooking and stuff as you all need it."

Taking her small hand gently in his big one; Bob gingerly squeezes back. "Uh…my names Robert Calvin, most folks call me Bob, and my Mama is Ms. Henry. If you want I can take you upstairs and show you the place." Bob is blushing, and acts as if he has never been ask to shake a woman's hand.

"Well Robert Calvin better known as Bob, let's go meet your Mama."

I watch them walk away, and dismiss Hal and the others…no reason to guard the doors now.

Walking over to Johanna, I pause.

I move my right arm, and am curling my fingers under her chin forcing her to look into my eyes. "Johanna, don't make me a failure in keeping you safe."

I watch her take a breath, and then, her lips move. "I'm sorry. I also am extremely grateful for the pure goodness and generosity of your heart and your spirit. I know we cannot save them all, but saving her and that baby…that could mean entire generations of a single blood line will go on."

After the way I handled her earlier, I'm unsure what to do next. She bites her bottom lip. Her hands are moving through my hair as she gently pulls my head down. Her soft lips move against mine in a long lingering kiss. She relaxes her hold. "Michael, I like to be kissed in a manner in which I can participate." I smile, take her into my arms, and again we kiss.

Before things go any farther, in apprehension, I release her, and take her hand. "This is not the place I imagine doing anything for the first time. Besides I'm starving, let's go up to the apartment."

"I can cook, Michael."

I smile over at her as we wait for the elevator. "I bet you can, and I have the utensils and cookware needed to perform the task."

Within no time, the comforting aroma of rosemary fills the air. The chicken, rice, and asparagus look delicious.

"Wine?" I ask.

"Please."

I take out a couple of stems and pour the wine. She has set the plates on the kitchen bar, so we can eat casually. I feel her watching me in anticipation of my first bite. I smile as I cut a small portion of the chicken and place it in my mouth. I nearly choke as I realize she is watching me chew, awaiting my compliments. The taste is magnificent and literally melts in my mouth, but I say nothing as my utensils return to my plate to snatch another bite. Still, she watches and waits.

Three bites later, I ask. "Johanna, are you going to eat?"

She glares at me with a jovial contempt, and takes her first bite.

"By the way, this is the best rosemary chicken I have ever eaten. There is something different about it." She shakes her head and smiles.

"More wine?"

She looks puzzled. "Maybe not."

"You are welcome to anything I have."

Her eyes widen to smile at my revelation. "I don't want to get

91

sleepy; I fear soon we will begin to feel very weary."

I swallow hard, I had momentarily forgotten. In a friendly silence, we finish our meal. Without James we move to clean-up. Johanna carries the dishes to the sink as I load the dishwasher. Once we finish the dishes, I begin to think about the long hours ahead as we struggle to stay awake.

"I haven't seen James all morning, where is he?"

"James and one of the maintenance employees went to check on family members. It will take them a while. I don't expect them back anytime soon."

Chapter 9

Johanna Mueller

I am staring at a man standing on the balcony outside his high-rise apartment. He is entranced, staring out into the darkened day over a city he loves; a scientist that owns the knowledge of what is to come, and all that is at stake, a man, literally plagued by the baring weight of truth for all of mankind. He thinks I do not know what is happening, but I do. I knew when he came to my house to rescue me. I understood as predicted the day had come when our beloved sun would fail us for the first time. Of course, he knows what it all means in the grand scheme of science, all the cause and effects of the situation, and I simply can't comprehend how that must feel.

I gaze at him from behind the glass. Dr. Michael Levine, my knight, a man I met only a few days ago. The man wearing the face that might be the very last I see on this Earth. My affections for him are growing stronger with each passing moment.

A man's man, he's strong, confident, and wears his all too grumpy exterior well. I imagine many find his overall distinguished looks and no nonsense demeanor intimidating. For some reason, I do not.

Slowly, I open the door and join him. I notice the atmosphere is deteriorating. The air feels heavy exaggerating the smells of the city. I'm trying hard to suppress the cough threatening to escape my lungs.

Michael knows I am standing behind him, but he doesn't budge. His broad shoulders are straight and oh so rigid. He is so tense right now, and I am longing to do something for him. In a whisper, I ask. "What will happen next?"

He hesitates with his back still turned towards me. His answer shocks me beyond anything I know how to describe. "I want to make love to you."

My face is so hot; I can't imagine how red it must be. "Why?" I need to know if it is because I am currently the only woman available or he truly wants to make love to me.

His dry voice is hoarse. "I wanted to from the beginning that night at the beach when we went to Julio's, before the agents destroyed the evening, I knew. I don't remember ever wanting anything more."

I gasp. I don't even want to think of how undignified I might seem if I tell him how much I have thought about it. Well, it would be lewd. I know he is waiting for my response, but I am genuinely speechless.

I reach out, and gently touch the back of his shirt. He moves around to face me. I carefully smooth back a stray strand of hair from his forehead. His jaw is tight and the expression on his face is serious.

Our gaze locks, we stand without blinking. He is reaching for the door and opens it. My hand in his, he's leading me through the great room and beyond to his bedroom. Behind closed doors he renews his gaze into my eyes.

He is magnificent; the truth is I would have made love with him that night, after the beach. All he had to do was ask. Of course, Michael doesn't really ask permission. He says what he wants and the right to refuse is apparent, and if I need etiquette, I won't find it in Michael Levine.

He's still staring at me and I'm not sure what I should do. Suddenly, a flash of the disaster is before me, and I ask, again. "The conditions outside are dwindling, what is going to happen?"

He draws me closer into his chest and he's stroking my hair. "I want to make love to you; we can talk later. We aren't young, we know by now what we want. I want you."

I wrap my arms around his waist. He kisses my hair. I close my eyes as his hands are rolling down my sensitive sides. He grasps my waist and is walking me backwards to the edge of his bed. He sets me down and steps back. Balancing on one foot at a time in front of me, he removes his boots and socks. He drops down into

95

a kneeling position before me and looks at me with heavy sexy eyes.

"Johanna, you are so beautiful." If the moment wasn't so serious, I think I would be laughing.

His hands resting on my thighs, he's situating his body between my legs. My breath quickens as the tickling light touch of his fingers ascends my arms and neck. His sweet touch stops at the nape of my neck. His firm grip is massaging me as he steadies my head. His wet mouth is parting, and he is tasting my lips. It's erotic.

I'm feeling him sucking my bottom lip in as he bites it ever so slightly, I begin to quiver. His mouth moves, erotically caressing me, and he speaks. "Are you okay, J?"

J? "Yes." I gasp.

His tongue moves into my mouth and he tastes of white wine and rosemary, it's still delicious. His motion slides across my teeth. WOW! I take a deep breath and his hands slip to grip the hem of my blouse. The tiny touches I feel against my naked skin tickle. In one quick move, my top is gone and I'm sitting in my bra as Michael stares at my breasts.

A soft moan escapes him, and he begins planting soft teasing kisses across my chest. The man is without mercy. He slides his hands beneath my bottom and raises me off the bed. He kisses me

96

as his fingers undo the snap and zipper on my jeans. In unison with him, like a harlot, I unbutton his shirt and slide it off his shoulders. I possess no restraint; with one finger I trace the tiny trail of hair down to his zipper. He slides my jeans down to the floor and rises. I look at him and return the favor. I gasp when I realize what I have done. Oh, my goodness, I took it all off of him. I have him totally naked before he has shed me of my bra and panties. I'm looking at him, and he is gorgeous.

We both step out of our jeans. With one hand he whisks away the duvet leaving it in a mound at the end of the bed. Still standing, his fingers trace my spine several times. I'm shivering, and he is unsnapping my bra. The straps fall halfway down the length of my arms. Sort of in a hurry, I rush the progression by straightening my arms and letting it fall to the floor. He leans over and torments each with his tiny sucking kisses. Longing for even more of his attention, I press them firmly against his lips. The often abrasive man is more than accommodating.

A breathy "Michael" escapes me as his tongue descends the center of my belly. He tilts his head up, and in equally breathy words, he says. "I want you so much."

I feel as if my knees are going to buckle. I think he senses my weakness and grips my bottom. Using his palms, he massages it and assures. "I've got you…I'm not going to let anything happen to you." Again, I gasp as he grips my panties. Wasting no time, he's sliding them off, and is kissing me where they used to be. If I wasn't before, I'm losing it now, I feel faint. Thank goodness, he lays me across the bed.

Chapter 10

Michael Levine

Johanna rests her head on my chest with my arm curled around her. Radiating in the luster of our lovemaking, I am stroking her naked back. I found something awesome in the midst of what society will soon describe as the apocalypse. Unimaginable pain and suffering outside, and I just shared an indescribable experience with a woman. Perhaps it is the disaster, but it was never this incredible, not even with Sabine.

I smile softly as Johanna's finger doodling circles across my chest. She lifts her head and plants an innocent little kiss against my lips, and then returns her head to the resting position. It's as if neither of us wants to break away from what we shared for fear it will lead to the reminder of the sorrow the world is enduring.

She lifts her head to smile at me. "We will never know."

"What won't we know?"

"Whether it is the disaster or we just make good pillow partners."

I chuckle. "Why, was it a one-time event for you?"

She smirks at me. "That is not really what I meant."

I place my hands under her arms and lift her onto me. "I want to do it more. I want to do it a lot more."

She smiles. "Imagine, and coming from a grumpy man like you?"

I return to the apartment, the situation beyond our controlled environment is grim. I pause staring at the scene Johanna is painting. It is an exact replica of the mysterious fog I experienced during my hallucination.

I interrupt. "What is that?"

She twirls around on the stool, flushing, she smiles shyly. "I know it looks rather twisted like something created by an unbalanced personality, but in my dreams I passed through a shaft and this is what I saw."

I swallow the lump in my throat, and decide not to tell her it is the same vision I had when I dozed off. "No Johanna, I think it's excellent, your work is fascinating and it must sell for a healthy price."

She turns a brilliant red, and softly remarks. "Michael, I have never sold a painting."

I smile. "I know, but they could sell."

"Forget my paintings. You appear as the bearer of devastating news. What happened?"

"Despite my preparations here, we may need to leave the city. I'm just not sure when, but the death tolls are rising and disease is going to be rampant for a long time after the effects of the wave pass over. Three days without the presence of the sun means photosynthesis is non-existent. All plants in an active state of growth will die. The shortage of food and supplies will result in a famine like the world and especially the United States has never known." I watch as her eyes are filling and she is struggling to hold back the tears.

"Where will we go?"

"I have a place in New Mexico. It is getting there that is cause for concern."

She stands, and begins pacing, drowning in agitation. "Michael, go, I'm so stupid, I just realized I'm keeping you from everything, NOAA, safety and God knows what else. Please, go without me."

I roll my eyes and look up at the ceiling. "What in the Hell are you talking about. I would no more leave you than I would slit my own wrists. So stop it, right now!" Exasperated, I exit to the kitchen.

She puffs and follows me. I'm making another pot of coffee.

"Michael, you grumpy control freak, eventually you will have to tell me what you know." She turns leaving me.

I call after. "Yeah, and eventually you will have to tell me what the HELL it is your hiding."

I think as I am pouring the water into the coffee machine's reservoir. It is true; I will have to share the gut wrenching facts with her. At least until James returns, I'm not going to tell her a damn thing, but instead, enjoy her guarded innocence.

She catches me watching her from across the room. "Okay Levine, In case you have forgotten, we slept together, an intimate sort of occasion. I would appreciate just knowing what it is you do for a living."

I grin at her clever sarcasm, and remove a device from atop one of the tables. "Here catch." I toss the device to her; she catches it. "The son of a brilliant patent attorney, I learned early from my Dad. I patented everything when I worked full-time in the field. I now, manufacture tools, devices, and technology used by scientists from a variety of disciplines. The instrument in your hand is my latest. It is a remote sensing device used primarily by archeologists. It measures the moisture of manmade structures that lay hidden underground. Due to the porous nature, the older the structure or artifact is the more moisture it contains. It tells the user where to dig first. MLE designs nearly every piece of specialized scientific equipment on the market."

"Dare I say I'm impressed?"

I laugh loudly. Her next question leaves me puzzled.

"What kind of manufacturing capacity do you have, say for a single item needed by the masses?"

I am squinting at her through my wire framed glasses. "I don't know, but regardless, I do know how to get things done. Why do you ask?"

She shrugs. "Curious." A visitor wanting access prevents me from prying any further into her peculiarities.

I return with a husky man dressed in riot control gear. "This is agent Todd McCafferty. He was sent by Jenkins to check on your well-being."

Johanna stands and holds out her hand. "Thank you Michael, but I am acquainted with agent McCafferty." She turns her gaze back to the agent. "Hello Todd, as you can see I'm doing fine, and compared to others out there it feels almost vulgar to be living this well."

I stare blankly at her until I catch Todd's telling glimpse. "I understand; Jenkins wants you to talk to her alone. I'll be in my study, come see me before you leave." There is something familiar about agent Todd McCafferty; I can't quite put my finger on it.

After a brief exchange with the man in my study, I walk agent McCafferty to the door, and return to Johanna. One look at her and the vision of that night at the beach is flashing through my mind. "J, McCafferty, he's the one that carried you off that night at the beach, isn't he."

Johanna mutters. "Yes." I make eye contact with her and shrug.

<<<<<<>>>>>>

James Barone

What a day this has been, I am bone weary and heart sore. Standing in the corridor gazing at my key ring, I can't make up my mind which to do. My mind is foggy from lack of sleep, the sights I have seen, and the worry of what is to come. Where am I going? Oh yeah. Work or relax? I should go on back to my place and just take a nap! No, I can't, Michael says sleeping is dangerous now! That leaves my second option; cleaning and ironing. The world may be coming to an end or at least the world as we know it, but I cannot shirk my duties.

Boss may tease me about my job description, but we both know I am indispensable! Cleaning will certainly keep me awake, and I really have no idea how long the power will hold out; best to get things done now. The smoothly oiled door doesn't make a sound as I unlock it and step inside.

Entering this apartment has always been a secret pleasure of mine. I find that keeping this place sparkling allows me to share vicariously in its ownership. The lavish feel of the supple leather under my fingers as I straighten cushions, the slick gloss of the polished wood of the sideboard; gleaming beneath the lemon oil I apply so carefully once a week…what's that?

"Damnit, he left another water mark on the sideboard! Why can't he use a coaster like a civilized man?"

Muttering beneath my breath is a habit my mother would not approve of, but my mother never had to put up with the arrogant Michael Levine!

No matter how much I rub the mark with a soft towel from the front drawer of the sideboard, it persists in its ugly state. This mark will require a trick; a little mayonnaise should do it.

Looking around the room I spot a few other glasses and plates, gathering them up I make my way to the back of the apartment, to the kitchen.

After automatically loading the dishwasher…I immediately unload it. While the generator system should be enough to keep the entire building up and running; I am hesitant to test its power of longevity.

As the sink fills with hot, bubbly water…the sound of my pinky ring tapping against the plates sends me back to my childhood. With my eyes closed I can almost hear my mother's voice as she washed the dishes after dinner, and talked to me of…shoes and ships and sealing wax…of cabbages and kings…

Funny…I haven't thought of that in years. It is at times like this I miss her the most. Not on holidays or special days...but on the days when, if I admit it; I am frightened and unsure of what is coming. Her soft Italian voice always reassured me that no matter the evil that faces us, there was good on the other side.

The feel of the water dripping on my feet brings me back to the present! With a quick twist I turn off the water to the over-flowing sink... standing up sleeping! I am tired. Laughing to myself at the sorry mess I have managed to make...thankfully no one is here to see it! Damn, now I will have to mop!

With my routine down pat, it does not take me long to finish up the kitchen, and lay out the meat we will be having for dinner. With a last look around the kitchen, I think I will go straighten up the small office suite attached to the apartment; I haven't touched it in days.

Humming to myself, and not expecting to meet anyone, I am startled by the presence of a large man...Reaching for my sidearm is my first instinct, yet something about him is familiar...then I remember...Michael said he was bringing in extra security. That's the answer! Relaxing my stance, I smile and decide to make him feel welcome.

"Hello...I wasn't expecting to find anyone in here; you must be one of the new security men. I am James; can I help you find something?"

"I wasn't expecting to meet anyone in here. I thought you had your own place?"

"Oh, I do, I just came in to pick up the place a little." I replied.

"That's too bad."

Not the reply I expected, and it floors me for a moment. "I beg your pardon?"

Before I can fully react, the man moves quickly across the room, pulling a gun he slashes the barrel across my face, the shock of the hard blow lays the skin open from my left eyebrow to my chin. The pain is immediate and I can feel myself losing consciousness. As my knees buckle, he grabs me and throws me over his shoulder in a fireman's carry. This causes the pain to worsen so drastically that my mind gives up the fight to remain awake.

Sharp claws are tearing at me! Stinging and biting… this must be one of those dreams Michael warned me about! I have to wake up; what's that sound? Who's whispering? Who's moaning?

Why can't I open my eyes? There…one is open…the pain isn't stopping…this is no dream! Who's that? Shadowy and blurry…it's a man…clearer now.

"Good your awake, we can start now." The cheerful nature of the voice belies the coldness I can see in the face of my attacker.

With a quick look I realize we are in the basement…in

Michael's collection room. When I try to speak the pain burns through my torn face...the haze returns and I am about to pass out once more. Ignoring the pain and concentrating on understanding I ask;

"Who are you, what do you want here?"

"Let me explain how this works. I ask the questions, you answer them. Wrong answers or answers that do not please me will result in serious amounts of pain on your part. I will of course let you go... as soon as I have what I came for. Do we understand each other?"

Most people seriously underestimate me, I can't blame them...it is a notion I have fostered over the years...appearing less threatening allows me to get close and act quickly when it has been called for... I may appear to be the perfect gentleman's, gentleman...a bit slow on the uptake, and quite often teased about my proper dress code, and my constant nagging of Michael to be nicer and more understanding of others.

But I'm no fool...I know I'm not going to leave this room alive. I also know I will never give this man what he wants...no matter what that is. I nod yes, but in my mind I gather the strength to hold on...Michael might come looking for me.

I now exist in a place where time has no meaning...minutes seem like hours and an hour has been an eternity. Each time I slip

108

free and step into that place where nothing can touch me…he drags me back with sadistic pleasure. Even if help arrived this moment…I would not leave this room a whole man…my body is being broken piece by piece and my mind follows closely…

Through my gritted teeth I tell him once more that I can't answer his questions! I don't know what he's talking about…I don't know where the files are…I never saw Michael or the woman hide anything…The pain of the broken bones in my feet and hands is a grinding flame of agony….

I can feel the blood dripping off my flesh from a hundred small cuts…the harsh bite of the knife digs once more into the soft flesh between my thighs…my life is flowing out onto the floor, and still he cuts and hits and hurts…

"Il mio ragazzo." Through the ringing in my ears, I hear the soft voice of my mother; she always called me that; 'my boy'.
Forcing one eye open...I can see her!
"Mama?"
"Come, come with me now, this place is not for you any longer." Even as I feel another digging cut from the knife…I reach out and take mama's hand…standing and walking away from the pain…

Chapter 11

Michael Levine

Relocating during the days of darkness and even for some time afterwards will be dangerous at best. My plans of keeping the woman safe from unsubs wanting some sort of knowledge she possesses is now a different game all together. For now, the enemy is much different, the darkness and all that it implies.

I need to figure out how she will travel in unconventional areas and survive in the conditions it requires. Oh and trust, she must trust me. I ponder, I need to know, and asking isn't reliable enough.

Redirecting, I turn my attention to the door outside the inner-office elevator. I answer "Nick?"

Nick glances over at Johanna. "Sir, it's James, umm...I think you better come outside."

Rushing to the door, my voice is commanding. "Don't even think of leaving this apartment."

I follow Nick as he leads the way down to the freight elevator to the basement.

"Is he hurt?" I ask.

Nick keeps walking. I grab his arm and pull him to a stop just before we enter the elevator.

"We were doing a security check...we found him there." Nick answers softly.

"How bad is he hurt?"

Nick pulls away and steps into the elevator. His face is pale and his mouth is drawn. When he looks into my face, I allow the horror of what I see to show...briefly.

I quickly step in beside him and punch the button.

In the basement...Nick takes my arm.

"Sir, maybe I should just tell you, and you don't have to see."

"He's my friend, I owe him this..."

Nick releases me, and leads me down the hallway to the small room used for keeping my collection of antique weapons.

My heart sinks...

Opening the door allows the smell to escape. Warm blood...urine...

Stepping over the threshold, I can see James' body slumped in the chair. The dark blood is pooling beneath him...and has run across the floor.

"Find him." Is all I say as I walk over and place a shaking hand on the top of James' head...

Johanna Mueller

The distant sounds of sirens never ceases now. Screams drift up from the streets below…wails and crying are our constant companions. Standing on the balcony, I allow the sounds to wash over me. It would be easy to step back inside and close the doors and block out the sounds; but I feel I should bear witness to the dying and suffering of those below.

Michael is somewhere in the building checking on James…the look on Nick's face does not bode well. I envy Michael …his stoic control never slips; I hope James is okay, but I fear the worst..

In the distance, I can see others like me…standing on balconies high above the chaos, back lit by muted lights. Do they wish as I do that it was possible to open the doors and welcome all who would enter? Or are they satisfied in doing nothing and block the doors and save only those within?

That man in the blue robe is leaning against the railing sipping coffee as if this is a normal time. He appears relaxed and immune to the sounds that rake so harshly against my skin.

There…a woman paces back and forth…back and forth, stopping now and then to peer over the balcony railing. Is she searching for someone down there? Waiting for a husband who never came home or a child lost in the darkness teeming so heavily around us? Does she feel as I do that we have taken the high-ground with our superior security and belief that we are doing the right thing?

Down below me I think of the other refugees tightly encased within the walls of apartments Michael has given them. Is the young mother and her baby alright? Suddenly, I have to know…and despite Michael's orders to stay inside I must know and it has to be now.

Slipping through the semi-darkness of the apartment, I search out a large flashlight, and carefully exit the apartment. The large elevator stands across from me, and with a soft ding its doors open when I press the silvered button.

Pushing the button marked number three causes the doors to close and a soft whoosh accompanies the movement down. It is a quick trip in this modern building…everything designed to operate in fast motion…nothing but the best for a man who has the money to afford it.

The opening doors reveal a fainter light in the third floor hallway than that which exists higher up…as if down here the power is not quite as it should be.

Stopping to listen…I hear faint sounds from the apartments…which one does Bob and the others share?

Walking down the hallway I finally pause before the door marked 3D…a soft knock and I hear someone approach the door.

I can feel them looking at me through the peephole, I wave and smile.

The sound of deadbolts and chains dropping, then a narrow crack appears as someone peers out. "Yes?"

"Sorry to be a bother...I am looking for the apartment of Bob...the security guard?"

"Oh, sure...it's 3K." The woman feels safe enough to step halfway out the door and point helpfully.

"Just go down to the end of the corridor and turn right, it's right there."

"Thank you... Do you have everything you need?"

"Oh yes, we brought food and water with us, and the apartments are fully furnished with linens and everything. The kids have been having great fun playing in all this space!" Her voice is light at first, then a sober expression falls upon her and she appears older than she is for a moment.

Her voice drops to a whisper..."I tried to get my sister and her kids to come with us. She said no, and now I can't reach them on the phone or anything. She's never been the nicest person in the world, but she's my sister." She gives me a 'You know how it is' shrug.

"I am sure they are fine, and as soon as this craziness is over you will find them." I answer reassuringly...lies trip off my tongue so easily these days. "I better go now. Be careful, and if you need anything use the intercom system to call. Michael has it being monitored constantly."

"Thanks I will…be safe yourself." I watch her slip once more into the grayness of the apartment and listen to her engaging the locks.

Stepping quickly down the hallway, I locate 3K just where she said it would be. This time my knock gets a quick answer, most likely due to a forewarning call from the lady in 3D.

"Hello there, Wanda said we were fixing to have company and I guess she was right!" The elderly woman's voice is friendly and holds a hint of the Old South. "Come on in." She invites with a wave as she steps back to hold the door open wider.

"Thank you, my name is Johanna, and I just wanted to check on the young woman with the baby…and you and your son of course!" I say casually as I step inside…just a friendly visit on a normal day! I can play this game, I need to.

"Oh they are fine…she's such a good Mama, Leigh is in the shower right now, and that little Monkey is sweet as she can be! Come on into the kitchen and I will make us some tea." Following the slow and careful footsteps of the older woman I realize she walks with difficulty, yet does not allow her infirmity to stop her from going where she wants to go.

115

"Have a seat at that counter thing there...this kitchen is bigger than half my house! Such a pleasure to work in it, and as long as we have power, I tend to enjoy all the niceties!"

Taking a seat as directed, I find pleasure watching her as she makes tea. No teabag...the real thing is soon seeping in a cozy covered teapot. I smile in momentary delight as she also brings over two cups and saucers so finely made...they are translucent.

"I see you appreciate a fine tea setting. I was born and raised in Savannah, Georgia; at a time when tea time meant something. I have held onto that custom while I lost so many others."

I listen carefully as she tells her story while we wait for the tea to seep.

From another room I suddenly hear the sound of infant laughter...Cocking my head, I listen to the musical sound.

"That's Monkey, since it went dark we have all been afraid to sleep cause of the dreams; but she just seems to dream of pleasant things. Like my Mama said; maybe babies play with the angels when they sleep."

"Have you had bad dreams Ms. Henry?"

"Call me Mabel, and no not so much. Longing and sadness are mostly what I get. I have lived a life with few regrets and maybe that's why.

We take turns watching each other and Bob and Leigh, they

116

have had a bad turn or two. Bob mostly takes it hard when the dreams are of when he was over in Iran a year or so back…bad things happen in bad places, and sometimes people are forced to do things they later regret."

Her words hit me hard; I have a few regrets of bad times in bad places…I dread the sleep time more and more.

With one last caress of the fine china, I place my now empty cup on the saucer, and rise from my chair. With regret, I bid this woman good-bye. "I better get back upstairs, never know when the power might go completely, and it's a long walk!"

Joining me as I move to the door, Mabel places her hand on my arm and I pause.

"Thank you for coming down, when this is all over you come see me, and we will have tea and maybe be able to laugh again like Monkey in there."

"I will, and thank you." Impulsively, I take her in my arms and the warm frailness of her body gives me comfort.

Stepping into the hallway I make my way back to the elevator. With movements as smooth as any fine-tuned watch it begins to rise and return me to the penthouse suite apartment.

A sudden sharp slam throws me to my knees as the elevator jerks to a stop and the sudden darkness swoops down upon me!

Fumbling, I reach for the flashlight and thumb the button…but

117

nothing happens. I shake it and slam it against the floor, still no light. The quiet of the elevator is oppressing, and the darkness bears down on me like a heavy blanket.

Crawling, I seek with my hands and fumble up the wall to the face plate that holds the emergency buttons and a phone. Pressing the receiver to my head, I try to feel out the raised buttons that activate the emergency dial system. I push all of the buttons one by one…nothing happens.

Then with a soft whine that accompanies flickering lights the elevator once more begins to rise. I hold my breath as I watch the numbers…14…15…it moves smoothly and I breathe easy. Putting the receiver back in place, I relax.

Then at 25 it stops…the doors open…there's no one there. I lean out and the hallways are empty. Why did it stop? Stepping back inside I push the button for Michael's floor…the doors do not close. What the hell?

As I raise my hand to pick up the receiver once more all the lights on the panel go dark…the lights in the hallway flicker off and on!

I step out of the elevator quickly…I do not want to be confined in that small place alone and in the dark! Looking around, I dash towards the doorway marked stairway exit. Just as I pull the door open…darkness descends once more. Once more I fumble the flashlight out of my pocket, and once more it is a futile attempt to generate light.

I hold out my hands and push my feet forward to the first step that will lead me upwards. Grasping the hand rail, I pull myself up to the next landing…the darkness is so complete…like a cave far below ground. The whisper of my shoes on each riser and the slow slide of my hand on the railing accompany each harsh breath.

I count landings as I move upwards, two for each floor as they twist and turn on each level. Finally, I reach the 29th floor and begin to feel like this will soon be over. Below me I hear the sudden clang of a door shutting. Someone has entered the stairway below me.

Leaning against the railing I pause and listen…yes footfalls, heavy steps are climbing the stairs.

"Hello…who's there?" I call down.

The steps stop…yet there's no answer.

"I know someone's there…please answer me!"

The only sound is a sudden flat sound of someone now rushing up the stairs beneath me.

Frozen for a moment…now I panic as I turn and try to move as quickly as I can to the next landing…what floor is this? I can't remember. My hand slaps the railing as I spin around the next landing…can't stop…keep moving…the steps are closer…

Closer now I can hear them beneath me...maybe two landings separate us...I rush forward and upward into the darkness...31! It has to be this one...I leave the stairs and move where I think the wall should be...a hard knock as my hands slap the hardness of the wall! Fumbling along the wall I feel the doorway...and as I reach it, the steps hit the landing behind me and I freeze...stop breathing and press myself against the door.

I can hear them breathing near me, fast breaths...then a slide of a foot as they move forward...

I scream when a hand reaches out of the darkness and brushes my back...pulling the useless flashlight from my pocket I turn and raise it to use it as a weapon...and the lights come on.

Michael!

"Why didn't you answer me?" I plead in a whisper...my fear drains out of me leaving me weak and barely able to stand. He just looks at me. What is wrong with him?

I start to reach out to him...but he steps back...the look on his face...I drop my hand and simply stare at the face of a stranger...a stranger who hates me...what have I done that makes him look at me this way. Then beneath the anger and hatred I see the deep sorrow. James.

Michael Levine

My face feels red amongst the bruises I've been wearing since that night at the beach; moisture is pilling against my skin. The devastating sight of James' body instilled within me forever. I am looking at Johanna through darker eyes. Her expectancy now seems to change and she clearly understands something horrible has happened as sorrow is visibly invading her body. Instead of standing back in fear, she races to me, and throws her arms around me pulling me down towards her. I feel her hands moving in a deep caressing motion of comfort against my shoulder blades. I draw her into me and we stand in a long silent embrace.

My voice is hoarse. "Come on, I need a shower."

"Of course." She whispers.

I take her hand and lead her out of the stairway…no longer caring why she is there and not in the apartment. When I had first heard her above me in the darkness her voice had triggered an overwhelming urge to hunt her down and make her pay for James' suffering…for I am sure that her secrets are the reason he is dead…someone wanted something from James and were willing to torture him to get it.

Inside my bathroom, I take her into my arms again. My kisses are wet and determined as I smother her face with an anguish I am desperate to destroy. In fervor, I am removing her clothes. I am speaking in an impetuous voice. "J, you have to trust me like you

121

have never trusted anyone else in your life. Do you understand?"

Reluctantly, she nods.

I rip off my clothes, throw them across the floor and start the shower. Arms wrapped around her from behind, the water moves me into a trance-like state. She reaches for my shampoo and my hold loosens allowing her to turn around. My head drops and she is massaging the soap into a thick lather. She continues in a prolonging, soothing motion, kneading my head beyond necessity. Finally, stepping aside she allows the water to thoroughly rinse my hair.

I take the shampoo and squirt an excessive amount into the center of my palm, and return the favor. Not too rough, but still I am aggressive, massaging her hair and scalp with suds. I do this until I relax into a robotic repeating motion as I mindlessly sculpt forms, and shapes in her hair.

As I silently play with her hair, Johanna washes me with the liquid body soap from the ledge. I curve my head back and moan as her hands and fingers massage my body and hope the hot shower water is masking the escaping tears.

Chapter 12

Johanna Mueller

Michael has put the building in an energy conservation mode. It is a little stuffy, so I'm putting on a loose fitting sundress. I dry my hair. He still hasn't told me exactly what happened to James, and I know my fears of the worst are true. The strange CEO is not a master communicator, but I can see him drowning in the darkest region of human despair, grief amplified by guilt.

Entering the great room, I find him standing as if he is waiting for me to enter. Since returning, his mood is dark yet passionate. I don't understand the opposing sides, but my affection for him seems without boundaries. We are moving into the night time hours at the end of the first day of darkness, I realize the disaster has me behaving in a manner unlike my normal self. I am no longer worried about the driving force behind my emotions for Michael.

I am looking at his incredible body as he is moving near me, wearing soft pajama pants without a shirt. I'm like a young girl, I feel weak at the knees. I know he's reaching out to me from a painful deafening darkness, but it's okay. He needs to be filled-up and I want to be the one to fill him. I don't know what will happen. Are we bonding through our weaknesses or our strengths?

Most relationships fail because people often bond through their weaknesses instead of strengths. Can a relationship begin on unhealthy terms and emerge into something healthy when the darkness is gone? I don't know. Michael is grabbing my arm and pulling me into him, enveloping me. His entire being is wrapping around me. It feels so good.

"J, I need something from you."

"Of course, I will do anything Michael, what do you need."

"We need to practice."

"I don't understand." The stress is taking over his sensibility.

"I need to understand your fears. I have to know you will trust me." He's serious, but how can I prove this to him.

"I trust you Michael and I can tell you my greatest fear is a failure on my part that gives the wrong person access to important information."

"This is about us, you and me that's all. We will likely have to move to evacuate the city, otherwise I can't keep you safe from your predatory unsub or the impending deterioration of the city. You have to do what I say without question."

I'm looking at him through squinted eyes. "Okay Michael, I will. We made love, I trust you." I know it isn't the same for most men, but I wouldn't sleep with a man I didn't trust. He quits

124

talking and seems exasperated. Perhaps I'm dense, and my ignorance is frustrating him.

He's handing me a cup of coffee from a nearby table. "Drink this." No argument there, I need all the help I can get to stay alert.

I'm finished with my coffee and he is approaching me from behind. His arms are wrapping around me just under my breasts, and he is placing tiny light kisses against my neck in the sensuous area near my ear. I'm opening my neck to him enjoying the sensation. The tingles are spreading though out my body and a noisy sigh is escaping me.

He's whispering in my ear his voice is sexy and wanting. "Trust me."

"Oh I do Michael, I do." My eyes are closed and I feel him removing one of his arms from around me. A soft fabric is brushing across my face. I'm opening my eyes to see, but I can't. He is blindfolding me. "Michael!"

"Trust me; you have to learn to rely on me."

I cannot hide the concern in my voice, I'm afraid. "What are you going to do to me?"

"I told you, I have to know you trust me."

I gasp. "Does it really require a blindfold?"

He doesn't answer. Oh my God, what if Michael is the one I should be running from? Could Jenkins and I both be wrong?

Warm tears are touching the tops of my cheeks under the blindfold. The friction is wiping and the fabric absorbing. Michael isn't noticing or worse he doesn't care. Gripping my hand, he's leading me away.

With my free hand, I reach out to find his face and before I know it, I'm slapping him hard. He grabs my wrist and places it at my side without breathing a word.

I feel his breath against the right side of my neck. "Remember what I said." I'm so angry I push him away.

Now, he's holding my wrists firmly in his hands, leading me and coaxing me to sit. I recognize the cool leather of the curvy sofa against my bare skin. He is sitting next to me and wrapping his left arm around my shoulders, his hand is gripping my left shoulder. My breathing is heavy. I am scared to death.

He is pulling me down, I'm lying on the sofa and he is hovered over me. I can hardly move. Oh my God, what is he going to do now? My heart is palpitating; his fingers are floating across my bare shoulder blades. I'm sensing he is reaching for something and I'm holding my breath.

Something round and cold is ascending from my cleavage. I shiver. He's moving it up my neck and holding it against my lips. I'm not opening. He is rolling it around my lips in tiny circles. He wants me to open my mouth. Out of fear, I'm responding by

126

parting my lips slightly and my tongue is inspecting the surface. Cold, smooth, and elongated round, firm but it has some flexibility.

"What is it?"

Fear has left me demented, unable to think. I am acting like a child or maybe a pet. I'm sticking my tongue out in defiance, but he is accepting it as compliance. He is rolling the object across the surface of my tongue. Out of a gag I say, "Grape." He is pushing it into my mouth with what feels like his index finger. The fruit inside, his lips and tongue are invading mine. I am not reciprocating.

He is taking my hand in his, moving me several steps left and forward from the sofa, we stop. "Walk around the room at a moderate pace... and keep your hands to your sides and understand I'm here."

"Michael!" I'm panting like a helpless puppy.

"Do it!"

I'm taking a couple of small steps, moving forward, I'm stopping, and I feel disoriented. "I need my hands, Michael please." I beg.

His voice is strong and very cranky. "Do it!"

I'm slowly shuffling my bare feet against the floor in a forward motion. He is calling out. "Turn right." Turning, I continue, but I am not picking up my speed. I'm walking and I know I'm going to run into the wall. My pace is slowing down to a tip toe. Suddenly, I'm crashing into him. I'm gasping, loudly. The jerk is wrapping his arms around me. "Pick up your pace!"

Taking off in a hurried march, I'm angry and Michael is spitting out orders. "Right, turn left…faster J…sense where I am." Stopping, I'm stomping my feet like a three year old. "Michael, I'm no good at this. Don't punish me."

Ignoring my pleas, he orders. "Keep going." Again and again he is alternating, directing me and having me slam into him. It's exhausting and I am confused. He's right, I should be able to sense where he is, but I'm failing.

Dropping to the floor, I plead. "Michael please, I beg you, stop." He's moving beside me on the floor, and I'm crying. He's lifting me, onto his lap, and cradling me.

He's shifting me; I'm sitting on his lap. His hands are wrapping around my wrists and he raises them. "Memorize my face with your hands." My hands are caressing his face. He's already removed his eyeglasses. I feel moisture. His face, his beautiful face, it feels so good, yet so sad.

He's removing my blindfold and I'm crying. On the table I see a plate of a variety of foods and realize to him this wasn't at all twisted. Rolling into a ball, I'm huddling into his chest.

128

He is stroking my back. "We'll try again later."

I am sobbing. "No Michael, I trust you as much as any person can trust another."

He's kissing my hair, but his voice is strong. "I need you to trust me beyond humanness." His hand is massaging my thigh just below my buttocks. I'm raising my right arm and curling it around his neck pulling his face next to mine. After everything he just put me through, I want him. My lips are moving over his face, covering it with wet desperate kisses. I pause in the midst of my wild passion. "Michael say something, I need assurance."

Our eyes meet. "I want you; I want you so much it hurts, and I must keep you alive. Someone murdered James."

Instead of crumbling my passion…his words send me seeking pleasure. Is that not what we do? Seek an assurance of life in the midst of death?

Michael Levine

Spent, I am rolling over onto my pillow. My breathing is heavy and loud. I am sure I just gave Johanna everything I had including what is left of my soul. I close my eyes and see flashes of James lying in his own blood. I don't remember what it's like to live without James; I open my eyes and glance over at Johanna, her head sweetly pressed against the pillow, she is staring at me. I can't lose her too.

She reaches for me. "Michael has there been a Mrs. Levine?"

After dreading this question since the moment I met her, I laugh loudly. She looks stunned. "No, she would not take my last name."

"Why, you seem honorable and successful. I guess I'm surprised."

Again, I'm laughing. "I guess that's one thing I can't blame her about; her name is Sabine, say it."

She smiles, "Sabine Levine?" She's laughing uncontrollably and I can't help, but join her.

"You loved her, do you still love her?"

"It was a long time ago, shortly after graduate school. I guess I did, but I don't anymore." Johanna leans into me and plants a quick kiss against my lips.

"What about you?"

She whispers. "I'm ashamed to admit, I was married, but I have never been in love."

"Do you have any children?"

She smiles, but quickly I notice tears are welting in her eyes. "I have an amazing grown son, but I failed at that too. Jenkins talked to him just yesterday, before the darkness, he's in Spain. I am so worried, after all of this...how will he get back to the states? "

I lift her onto my chest. "You didn't have a choice. You had to go into protection." Her warm tears are dripping onto my naked chest.

She takes a deep breath. "Before they put me in protection things were happening and my son thought I had suddenly become a paranoid crazy woman." She pauses. "I lost him several months before I went into the program."

I gasp and without realizing I let words slip out. "My God..., I'll do everything I can..."

She places two fingers over my lips. "Shhh, no promises." She rests her head back against my chest.

Chapter 13

It is the morning hours of the second day of darkness. I now despise the glass outer walls I have always enjoyed. I scoff at the thought 'you can see out, but they can't see in.' Now willing to trade the feature, I would rather them see me doing anything than see what is going on in the streets.

It's been hours since I was able to contact anyone on the outside. The feeling is eerie and I would surely be mad by now if Johanna was not with me. The compulsory isolation is strange and unnerving. Watching her and making love to her is my only solace, everything else is appalling.

I notice her standing in the doorway of my study. She is awesome, and holding up so well under the dark conditions of confinement. I shrug at myself; practice really does help in the worst of situations. Of course, I've had my own practice, but that's been several years ago, now.

"Come here." She moves next me.

I pull her onto my lap. Comfortably situated, she's wrapping her arms around my neck. I give her a half smile. Like so many times during the past hours my arms are encircling her. Already, I'm thinking about the next time we will make love. I take a deep breath and redirect my thoughts.

Is she ready for the journey that lies ahead? "We will begin our travels in about eighteen hours. We will be going to a shelter I built in New Mexico near Elephant Butte Lake." She's staring at me with a blank expression.

I'm brushing back her hair and kissing her neck. All the money I've made, all of the things I own and right now, I feel like all we have is each other. "Do you know how to use a gun?"

She sits up straight. "Yes, but I won't."

I didn't expect such a reaction from someone that had worked at the Pentagon. Tightening my hold, I kiss her again. "You must try, Marshal Law will break out if it hasn't already and the gun issue is no longer a fun thing to protest. Baby, it is the new way of life. At best when the sun returns, only the cities will have any type of government, outside there will be pockets of militia and anarchists. I expect in a very short period an all-out revolution will manifest." I feel her shiver. I know I need to be tougher with her, but I am becoming less effective with each passing minute, a first for me.

I change the subject and the direction of the activity. "Are you hungry? I'm starving, I watched James enough, I know how to make omelets, let me make one for you." She smiles and nods and we head out of the study to the kitchen.

I open a bottle of wine. "Wine with omelets, why not?"

133

Johanna giggles as I pour the wine in a couple of crystal goblets.

I raise my glass and she mimics. "To us and our journey ahead." We clink our glasses together and drink.

Turning to the refrigerator, I remove some vegetables, eggs and cheese and begin chopping. She is giggling again. "Michael let me help you."

I smirk. "I thought you would never ask."

Again, we manage to find an activity that can keep us distracted from the reality lurking outside. It is imperative we stay active, and alert. Mentally sleep can inflict potentially deadly problems for the psyche.

Without much conversation, we prepare the food, and eat, genuinely enjoying the process. We both laugh as we realize we just finished two bottles of wine. Johanna is showing the effects of the wine making me laugh as we begin cleaning up. "Oh Michael, I might have drank too much."

I smile. "I know exactly what we can do to keep you awake."

She laughs. "Again?"

The ringing of the doorbell interrupts my playful stalking of Johanna. She giggles and waves bye-bye with her fingers. Walking over I see through the peep-hole that it is Nick.

"Nick, step inside."

Scanning the room, he pauses when he catches sight of Johanna. "Sir, I think you may want to step out here."

I nod, remembering the last time Nick asked me to step out, but I walk out, and shut the door. "What is it Nick?"

"Well sir, we need to further conserve energy. This will require us to shut down most if not all of our security and lights. Without solar renewal, we could lose all power before the sun returns and resources are available and stabilized."

My expression is grim, but I nod. "Do it." I look at Nick. "Is there something else?"

"Yes sir, it's about James."

I snap. "What about James?"

"Umm. Sir, I found this at the scene, I thought you would want it." Nick hands a photograph to me.

My eyes grow huge. It is a picture of Johanna stepping out of a cab at the Pentagon with a drawn sword piercing through her head. I look up at Nick, my tone is commanding. "Do not breathe a word of this to anyone. J and I will evacuate as soon as I think the time is appropriate."

Nick nods. "Yes sir."

"Now, go take care of the energy, blackout everything except the residences, you take the guest studio. No one goes into James' apartment unless I approve it. Do you understand?" Nick nods

135

and leaves me to my contemplations in the hall outside my residence.

I stare down at the photo, and realize this leaves little room for doubt. Johanna's secrets are the reason James is dead.

Inside the apartment I find her waiting with expectancy.

"Michael is something wrong."

I answer quickly. "Nothing unexpected, we are just going to cut the power on MLE. It will have no effect on the residence." Unable to hide her look of concern, she nods.

Looking at her through grim eyes, I ask. "What is it that your perpetrators want?"

She stares at me. "I really don't know and as you surely have already figured out, I'm a really horrible liar."

She has a point there. I raise my eyebrows. "Yes, I have noticed how uncomfortable you are with falsehoods. Nevertheless, I can't help, but feel as if you are a master at failing to divulge pertinent facts." Damn, I didn't intend for my words to appear as an accusation, but someone murdered James.

She's angry. "What are you suggesting?"

I don't back down. "From my vantage point the evidence suggests otherwise, and you can paint any picture you want, but the fact is you trust Jenkins about as much as I do."

She interrupts. "You self-righteous jerk, you don't know

anything. It is not Jenkins that I don't trust."

I roll my eyes at her. "If you would kindly let me finish, I was about to say that I understand. You had no choice, Jenkins was all you had, now, things are different, and you can trust me."

Quietly, she moves over to the sofa and sets with her hands clasp in her lap. She speaks softly. "The truth is I know a lot of things and they are not the kind of information you would expect a Pentagon researcher to know. I never worked on matters that dealt with weapons or military intelligence. Always assigned to obscure projects, I worked alone. Any one of the hundreds of assignments could interest someone. I cannot ascertain which of them has someone threatening my life." I am rubbing my face with my hands. "Michael I'm sorry. It's okay. I understand this is more than you bargained for."

I snap at her. "I didn't say that."

She whispers. "You didn't have to."

"I'm just trying to make sense out of the situation. It isn't a negotiation."

She's moving towards me with a strange look. Stopping next to me, I feel her breath. "Sure it is; everything is part of a negotiation, Michael."

I look down at her half-drunk from the wine and unbuttoning my shirt. She moves quickly pushing it over my shoulders and down onto the floor. I stand as the determined woman undoes the snap and unzips my jeans. Her hands slip beneath the waist of my jeans and boxers and she yanks them down to the floor. I am standing naked and stoic in the great room of my apartment. She coaxes me down on to the floor and pushes me to lay flat. "What about you, Dr. Levine?"

I chuckle. "What do you mean…what about me?"

"You want me to trust you, but the real issue is you don't trust me." I lay silent, but realize she is very serious.

She straddles me and presents the same blindfold in front of me that I used yesterday to cover her eyes. "Let's see how much you trust me. Dr. Levine, how well do you operate in the dark?"

I stare at her through cold eyes. "I think you missed the point, Johanna. The trust I am concerned about will keep you alive. I want to keep you with me and alive. As for the dark, I am more than familiar with it. I wear these glasses, because I spent two months in the dark without seeing even a glimpse of the light of day. It seriously damaged my eyesight."

Obviously stunned, she sits silent mounted atop me, but eventually I see my declaration is not going to stop the woman and her mission. She removes my glasses and sets them on top of the table next to her, leans over me, and blindfolds me. "Prove it."

I take a deep breath refusing to allow her to see my mounting anxiety. Unable to see, I feel her tongue as it traces my lips. "Michael, I need to know you trust me, and it is every bit as important as you knowing I trust you. Show me, you trust me." Confused, I don't react. I feel her weight lifted from my middle, and hear her leave. Stark naked flat on my back in the middle of the room, she leaves me, flashes of my experience in Yemen has me breathing heavily. Yemen…my worst nightmare might be responsible for saving our lives.

Why in the hell am I letting her do this to me? I have a choice, and I am bigger than her. Besides, it's no secret the last woman I trusted was Sabine, and look where that got me. My wife fell right into the arms of some damn European Casanova. Since Sabine left, I haven't even pretended to trust a woman, at least not in a relationship.

After several long moments, I feel the vibrations of Johanna's bare feet as she steps towards me. She sits next to me. Her hands are moving in a soft caressing motion around my chest. Hoping she doesn't turn her head to see my body reacting, I remain still. What did she have in mind, tormenting me with sex? I want to laugh, but I will refrain.

She whispers. "You didn't remove the blindfold and move. Perhaps, you do trust me a little or you care enough to make me believe you do. I've seen what I need to see, but know your explanation about your eyesight saved you and I'm letting you off easy. Don't think that will always be the case." She climbs back up on my middle and grasps my wrists. I'm puzzled; didn't she say she saw what she needed to see? "Having admitted all of that…well, I want to know if you can do this with me in complete darkness."

Wiggling her body, she positions herself closer to my chest, and places my hands on her waist. I squeeze her sides before grabbing the bottom of her blouse and pulling it over her head. Her hands against each of my cheeks she places her lips against mine and begins kissing me sweetly. I return her kiss, but with considerably more passion.

She frees herself from my embrace, straightens and stands above me and lets her skirt fall down on me before returning atop my chest. My hands quickly make their way up her thighs in a massaging motion, no panties, continuing up, my fingers ascend to her breasts. She's still wearing her bra. I reach my arms behind and unsnap her bra, pull it down her arms, and then throw it across the room.

She grabs my shoulders and coaxes me into a roll. Stretched out, above her, still blindfolded, I whisper. "What is it about you?" I can't see her, but I know she is smiling.

"Show me, Michael."

Chapter 14

I stroll around the apartment and look into the guestroom, but don't see Johanna. Running out of places, I peek into my room. I smile at her propped up on my bed reading a book. She looks up at me and returns my smile. Taking a deep breath in an attempt not to become distracted, I turn my attention and inform her of my plans. "I'm going to take a flashlight downstairs and retrieve some items for our trip. Nick is going to help me. Do not go outside of this apartment. Do you understand?"

She mumbles. "Yes."

In a move completely out of character, I approach her and place a kiss on her cheek. "Are you okay with that?"

She nods. "Yes Michael."

"Okay, I'll be back as soon as I can."

I meet Nick in the hall. "Boss, I turned on the power to the service elevator, I thought we would need it for the gear."

"Good thinking Nick."

We take the service elevator down thirty-one flights to the basement and exit the elevator at the bottom. We walk back to the storage room where I keep my field gear. Inside we pack backpacks with lights, rope, bungees, knives, and other necessities Johanna and I might need. I pick up a couple of boxes of meals ready to eat...MRES, the military answer to drive-thru;, and we make our way to the elevator.

Once inside I remember, we will need a couple of waterproof packs for Johanna's clothes. The facility is already equipped with clothes for me, but not for her. "Damn Nick, go on up, and unload the elevator, I'm going to grab a couple more things then I will meet you."

"Sure Boss." Nick replies.

I return to storage, open the box with the new waterproof bags, inspect them and take a moment to look around the room in case I am forgetting anything else. Satisfied that I thought of everything, I close the door and lock it.

I walk down the corridor to the elevator, hit the button, and wait. Nick should be finished removing the items we loaded earlier. I pace wondering if I should begin climbing the thirty-one flights of stairs up to the high-rise.

Looking up, prepared to begin my ascent, I notice the numbers above the elevator are beginning to show signs of descent. What a relief the alternative was not a pleasant thought. The doors open and I step in amongst several of the items Nick and I placed inside earlier. I insert my override key and press the button.

I push the button and the doors open on the twenty-ninth floor. I slip down the hall into my company office. I throw the

142

bags down I retrieved from storage, using the flashlight; I unlock the console behind my desk and remove a survival knife and my Glock.

The hidden stairwell that leads from my office to the study in my apartment is pitch black without even the tiniest hint of light. Unsure of what I am about to encounter, I creep up the stairs without making a sound. I stop at the door, gently I turn the knob leaving a small slit between the jam.

I hear a familiar voice interrogating Johanna. "Where did your boyfriend put the plans?" Agent Todd McCafferty! That son of a bitch!

Johanna cries out. "I don't know what you're talking about."

I grimace when I hear him smack her. She's sobbing. "Please, I can't give you what you want. You must know… tell me what you think I have."

McCafferty yells at her. "Where did he put your things?"

I plead under my breath. Come on J, tell him anywhere, so he will get away from you and I will know where he is…

She screams... I'm unsure about what he's doing to her. I slip through the door and crouch down behind my desk in the study. My God visions of James flash before me. I have to do something fast. The murderer now has Johanna!

She cries out again. "The formal dining room, Michael had

James put my office items in his dining room."

I whisper. "Good girl. Thank God."

"You better be right lady, I've had enough of you, Jenkins and that rich bastard trying to save the day. You know that device is worth more money than that arrogant son of bitch has already made, like hell if I'm gonna let him have it now, and with this darkness disaster it'll be worth more than ever."

I hear a loud thump. He's moving. I position myself to make way to her and watch as he strides across the great room. I slip around the corner. Tied to a chair, Johanna is badly beaten.

My hand-gun in position in one hand, I cut the rope holding her up with the other.

"Shhh." I pick her up and rush to the study to hide her behind my desk. I kiss her forehead, crouch down and race out and into the great room hiding behind the sofa. Scanning the room, I slide across the floor near the dining room entrance.
I slip and he sticks his head out the door. Suddenly, without warning McCafferty rushes out of the dining room and races to the door. I aim and shoot hitting the bastard in the shoulder.
I follow into the hall outside of the apartment, but I lose sight of him. Nick bound and gagged is somewhat delirious from a blow to the head. I free Nick and return to the study.

Johanna lay curled up on the floor behind the desk. Her face is red and badly bruised. I fall to the floor, lay down the gun, and pick her up raising her onto my lap.

I lift her head to mine and lean into her rocking as if she is a baby. "Oh God Johanna, I failed you."

Still looking out of it Nick steps into the study. "Boss, I'm sorry, he was waiting for me outside the elevator. How is she?"

"He beat the hell out of her. Now, go get me the first aid kit, wet washcloths and ice. Hurry!"

"Yes sir!" He yells as he rushes out of the room.

I push her hair away from her face. "Come on Honey…Talk to me!"

Out of a delirium, her whispers are weak. "How could he have known?"

Desperate and confused I ask. "How could he know what?"

Panting through the pain she speaks. "My experiment, the project papers…Cindy and Adam..."

"Baby, what experiment?"

She's drifting; I think of the perils of sleep during the darkness and realize I must bring her back.

"Come back to me, don't go to sleep." I look up as Nick returns.

"While I get her patched up…check on the others. Tell them to look out for Todd…he's bloody. Once you make sure the people are safe, get the vehicle loaded, we are leaving."

"Okay boss, but will she be okay to travel?"

"We can't stay here...tell everyone on the third floor to seal their doors. They will be safe, but I can't guarantee the power."

Nick rushes off while I gently bathe Johanna's wounds. I patch her up...and then force her to wake up and walk with me to the bathroom.

"You have to stay awake...tell me what he wanted that cost James his life and almost cost you yours."

"A small brown bag, it's in the box of paints, brushes and there's a canvas...James is not the only one who has died because of this. I don't want anyone else to die, Michael." She whimpers in pain and obvious self-loathing.

"Nobody else is going to die. We know who he is now, and we will be ready when he or if he comes back. Let's get you changed, and then we have to be moving on."

With Johanna safely behind the closed door of the bathroom, I can turn my thoughts to preparations'.

Nick is standing at the door waiting for me. I tell him to grab as many boxes of ammunition as he can carry, put it all in the front seat and then gather up the Kevlar vests from the security office downstairs and pack them around the windows in back of the Suburban. He hesitates before leaving and I am sure I am not

146

going to like what he says. I don't. It seems Todd got away.

I demand an answer. "How the hell did he get out of the building, that's what I want to know?"

"Sir, we don't know. We found a blood trail that led to the maintenance elevator, and searched on every floor, we found blood on the exit grates to the ventilation system on the roof."

"The fuckin' roof! What is he Batman? Where did he go from there?"

"Bob's mother said she thought she heard a helicopter earlier this evening. She had taken the baby up to the atrium."

"Holy…he could have killed them as well!"

"Yes sir, I have told them all to batten down the hatches until they can hear from you."

Inside, I'm chuckling…the dumb son of a bitch might have created and met his own death as the atmospheric conditions since the wave have created dangerous levels of fine air particles and unreliable air pressure zones, so much so that a helicopter or airplane journey is suicide.

"Okay…here's the plan. We are leaving and heading due west for New Mexico. Now I trust you, but nobody else. If you trust one man…bring him…if not we are on our own."

Without hesitation Nick says a name. "Bill Hoskins. He's the older guy who was with me when we found James. He is old-school sir. Shoot first, worry about the lawyers later."

"My kinds of man...go get him see if he wants to ride shotgun through the Old West!"

With a few swift steps I reach the bathroom door and bang on it. "Come on out of there, it's time to get this show on the road."

"Sir, what about the darkness...will we be able to drive safely? Not that I doubt your driving skills or anything, but you're no professional, I mean James was your driver."

"True enough. Well then let's see if your friend Bill will make you feel better by driving. I have no problem with him at the wheel Nick."

"Good enough." Nick closes the door.

Half an hour later we are in the parking garage, armed and ready to move out. With one hand firmly on Johanna's arm I rush her forward, she is clutching that damn brown bag like it's a lifeline.

Bill gets behind the wheel, and lays his Sig Sauer in his lap, three speed loaders rest between his legs. Nick is in the back seat with Johanna, and he carries a sawed off Greener.

I take shotgun position and carefully place an array of weapons around me. The back of the suburban has the windows barricaded with bullet-proof vests, only narrow openings are available for side viewing past the front seat.

From the driver seat we hear the gravelly voice of Bill as he speaks for the first time that I know of.

"Hope everybody went pee; this stagecoach don't stop till it reaches the end of the line."

We lock the doors, start the engine and slowly make our way out onto the streets where chaos rules.

Darkening Danger

Darkening Danger

151